Philippa Fisher
and the
Fairy's
Promise

ALSO BY LIZ KESSLER

Philippa Fisher's Fairy Godsister
Philippa Fisher and the Dream-Maker's Daughter

The Tail of Emily Windsnap
Emily Windsnap and the Monster from the Deep
Emily Windsnap and the Castle in the Mist
Emily Windsnap and the Siren's Secret

Emily Windsnap's Fin-tastic Friendship Book

Philippa Fisher
and the
Fairy's
Promise

LIZ KESSLER
illustrated by KATIE MAY

CANDLEWICK PRESS

Text copyright © 2010 by Liz Kessler
Illustrations copyright © 2010 by Katie May

First U.S. edition 2010

Library of Congress Cataloging-in-Publication Data

Kessler, Liz.
Philippa Fisher and the fairy's promise / Liz Kessler; [illustrated by Katie May].
— 1st ed.
p.   cm. — (Philippa Fisher ; 3)
Sequel to: Philippa Fisher and the dream-maker's daughter.
Summary: Philippa and her fairy godsister, Daisy, are asked by the High Counsel to go on a fantastic journey together to find a missing fairy and preserve the portals that connect the fairy and human realms.
ISBN 978-0-7636-5031-5
[1. Fairies — Fiction. 2. Friendship — Fiction. 3. Magic — Fiction.]
I. May, Katie, ill. II. Title. III. Series.
PZ7.K842Pl 2010
[Fic] — dc22   2010007560

10 11 12 13 14 15 RRC 10 9 8 7 6 5 4 3 2 1

Printed in Crawfordsville, IN, U.S.A.

This book was typeset in Hightower and Maiandra.

Candlewick Press
99 Dover Street
Somerville, Massachusetts 02144

visit us at www.candlewick.com

*This book is dedicated to Jenny —
because without you,
none of these books would have happened.*

*Thank you, Miss Richardson.
Wonderful English teachers like you
change the lives of unruly pupils like me.*

Fairy roses, fairy rings,
Turn out sometimes troublesome things.

— WILLIAM MAKEPEACE THACKERAY

BEFORE THE BEGINNING

The woods were deserted that day.

The stones stood still and silent, as though they were waiting for something. At the center of them all, a jagged piece of amber glowed in the growing darkness. Lights fizzed softly around it, turning pink, orange, purple, blue.

No one saw it. No one ever did. Why would they? No one knew about its magic, not anymore. They had forgotten all about such magic a long, long time ago. About the same time they stopped believing in fairies.

How foolish.

*   *   *

The boy grumbled to himself as he crossed the darkening woods. "It's not fair!" he muttered, panting as he clambered up the hill that lay halfway between school and home. It was mid-winter and the light was fading fast. The roads would have been quicker, but Tommy Williams preferred the woods, where there was no Danny Slater to trip you up and laugh at you on your way home.

Tommy's cheeks burned with anger and shame from Danny's latest bullying. It had been in the morning's gym class—but it could just as easily have been anywhere and anytime.

"*Wimpy Williams can't climb a rope! Wimpy Williams, what a dope!*" The taunt had followed him around all day, and now it had led him to retreat to the woods.

"I'll show him!" Tommy said out loud as he reached the stone circle that stood at the top of the hill. "I'm *not* a wimp, I *can* climb. I can climb better than *he* can!"

And with that, Tommy flung his school bag on the ground and made for the stone in the center of the circle—the largest of them all. He found his first few footholds easily enough, his toes poking into sharp holes in the side, his arms wrapped around the stone in a bear hug.

With a determination known only to those who have ever been desperate to escape the taunts of the Danny Slaters of this world, Tommy climbed onward, finding foothold after foothold. He pressed himself against the stone, felt around for crevices for his aching toes and burning hands. Breathless, filthy, and sweating, he finally grasped above him and felt the top of the stone. Mustering every last ounce of his strength, he heaved his body up, pulling himself to the very top of the stone. He'd done it!

Looking down, he laughed. "*Now* who's the wimp?" he shouted to the woods, his voice dying on the mist that was beginning to settle around him, along with the deepening darkness.

He clambered across the top of the stone, looking for a gentler route down than the sharp climb that had led him here. His parents would worry if he wasn't home before dark.

But then he stopped. Something was glinting at his feet. Something shiny among the gray that now seemed to envelop the whole wood. What was it?

He bent down and scrubbed at the moss and grime surrounding it. *This will prove I was here,* he thought. *Take this back to the class and tell them it's from the highest stone at Tidehill Rocks, and no one will call me tiny again!*

And so he scratched and scrubbed and pulled and heaved until, eventually, it came loose. It was like nothing he had ever seen, and Tommy was mesmerized. A shining, glistening piece of pure amber, it glowed and sparkled as he looked at it. It felt to Tommy as if he were holding pure magic in his hand.

"Wow," he said, staring at the jagged rock in his palm. As he held it, it began crackling and sparkling and lighting up like a fire.

Stunned and awed, Tommy held the rock carefully as he found an easier path down the back of the rock. Grabbing his school bag and throwing it over his shoulder, he glanced at the rock, now alive with color. It seemed to dance in his hand.

"You haven't ever climbed the tallest stone on the woods and found one of these, have you, Danny?" he asked out loud, laughing at the thought of the confrontation he imagined taking place the next day at school.

But there would be no confrontation the next day. And for Tommy Williams, there would be no school, either. Because the moment he walked through the gap in the stones to leave the circle, something quite unexpected happened.

Tommy, holding tightly on to his rock, took the step that divided the inside of the circle from the outside — and disappeared.

The woods suddenly felt colder than usual. The darkness hung more heavily.

The amber was gone — and now nothing would ever be the same again.

chapter one

Daisy

I'd been with the Admin and Liaison Department (ALD) for nearly two months when the news hit my screen.

To be honest, I almost missed it. Not because I wasn't concentrating—although I have to admit, ALD *is* the most boring department in the whole of ATC. (That's Above the Clouds, fairy godmother headquarters.) I'd been put here after what happened with Robyn's dad when he trapped me in a jam jar. My wing still wasn't back to normal since it had gotten crushed in the jar. But I was healing and couldn't wait to get back to doing real assignments again.

In the meantime, my job was to cross-reference fairy god-mothers with their departments and match them up with their clients. I could do it standing on one wing—provided it wasn't my bad one. So I hardly even thought about what I was doing. Punching in names, numbers, and departments didn't take a lot of concentration.

Which might be why I almost missed it when it came up on the screen. It wasn't one of my jobs to assign, so I couldn't see the details. But I saw enough:

JENNY FISHER. FGEAGLE5197. SRB.

SRB? No! I must be mistaken. I shut the page on my screen and walked across the office to the Clients file. I tried to saunter as casually as I could so no one would have any idea what I was doing. Interfering with an assignment from another department is strictly against Fairy God-mother Code. If I was caught doing it, I'd be in terrible trouble.

Luckily no one looked up. They rarely did. ALD is generally quite a serious bunch. There's a reason why the fairies here aren't out on normal assignments. Sometimes it's injury-related, like it was for me. Others are here because they're not up to par for any of the "live" assignments. Both of which helped give ALD the nickname Angry, Lonely, and Demoralized.

I grabbed the file of clients' records and looked up Jenny Fisher. I checked all the details from my screen against the ones in the file. It was definitely her. Philippa's mom. I went cold. Why was she getting a fairy from SRB?

I glanced around to make sure no one was watching what I was doing. Then I jotted down all the details of the assignment on the back of my hand, carefully replaced the file, shut down my computer — and ran out of the office as quickly as I could.

Philippa

"Are we almost there?" I asked for the twenty-fifth time.

Dad gave me the same response he'd given me twenty-four times already. "Almost!" he said, smiling at me in the rearview mirror and giving Mom a nudge in case she hadn't noticed his funny reply.

I sighed and got back to reading my book.

But then I noticed something outside the window. "Wait!" I sat up a bit straighter. "I recognize this road." I leaned forward and looked through the front windshield. "It's the woods!" I said. "We *are* almost there!"

"I told you we were," Dad replied.

"To be fair, you also said we were almost there when we hadn't quite reached the end of our street," Mom added.

But we were this time. We were on the outskirts of Ravenleigh. I felt a jiggle of excitement go through me. We were nearly at Robyn's house!

Robyn and I had met a few months ago when Mom, Dad, and I rented her family's former cottage for vacation. We'd kept in touch ever since, and she was one of my best friends now. The other one was Daisy. Daisy had been my fairy godsister (which is like a fairy godmother, only one that's the same age as you).

Robyn and I had had a rocky start — especially after her dad trapped Daisy in a jam jar and tried to cut off her wings. But once everything had settled down, he'd completely changed. He was like a different man and had ended up becoming friends with my parents. So well, in fact, that he'd asked if we'd like to come back to visit over winter break. They'd booked us into the same house we stayed in last time — their old home!

Unlike my other friend, Charlotte, whom I'd lost touch with since she moved away, Robyn and I had kept in touch since that week, e-mailing and texting each other virtually every day for the last three months.

We drove up the gravelly driveway as it was starting to get dark. It was only four o'clock, but the evening was closing in around us already.

"Can I go over to Robyn's?" I asked, swinging the car door open the second Dad turned the engine off.

"I was thinking we might at least make it through the front door first," Dad replied over his shoulder as he helped Mom out of the car, twirling her around and around.

"But I haven't seen her for ages!" I said, vaguely wondering what it would be like to have parents who could go longer than an hour or two without breaking into a dance.

"Let's get in and unpack first," Mom said, letting go of Dad's hands and opening the trunk. "Then you can run over to tell her we're here."

"Great!" I grabbed my bag and ran to the door. Minutes later, I'd squashed a week's worth of clothes into drawers, flung a bundle of books and magazines on the bed, and shoved my suitcase underneath.

"See you later," I called as I closed the door behind me and ran to Robyn's.

Robyn and I sat in her room above the bookshop her dad owns and caught up on all our news.

I couldn't help comparing it with what had happened when I'd gone to visit Charlotte the first time after she'd moved away. We'd spent a week not knowing what to say to each other. With Robyn, you couldn't shut us up if you tried! I don't know how we still had so much to talk about — but we did, and I wasn't complaining.

I checked my watch. Nearly six o'clock. "I'd better get going," I said reluctantly. Mom had told me to be back for dinner. "See you in the morning?" I asked as I headed down the stairs.

"Definitely! I'll come over as soon as I'm up."

"Great."

I was about to turn to walk through the shop to go out when something moving across the floor caught my eye. A mouse! It ran across the shop floor and right over to my feet!

I screamed and ran back to the stairs. The mouse followed me. I stumbled halfway up the stairs and the mouse tried to follow, but the steps were too steep and it kept falling back onto the floor.

It stood at the bottom of the steps looking up at me with tiny green eyes.

"I've never seen a mouse with green eyes," Robyn said. She'd heard me scream and was looking down from the top of the stairs.

"Me neither," I replied, although at this moment, I didn't care what color its eyes were; I just wanted it to stop chasing me.

"It likes you," Robyn said with a laugh.

"Well, I don't like it!" I replied. "Make it go away!"

"Look, it's got something in its mouth," she said, coming down the stairs, bending down and reaching out toward it.

"Don't touch it!" I screamed. Just then, the mouse dropped whatever was in its mouth, looked up at me once again, and scampered away.

I cautiously made my way down the steps as Robyn was examining what the mouse had left behind. It was a torn, crumpled-up piece of paper covered in mouse spit.

"Nice," I said.

Robyn laughed. She dropped the paper into the trash as we headed through the shop. "See you in the morning," she said at the door.

"Can't wait!" And with that, I waved to her and to her dad, who was busily chatting with a customer. And then I headed back to the house for an evening of moussaka and Monopoly with my parents.

The next morning, Robyn was at the door before Mom and Dad had even woken up. Which isn't that amazing, really. When Mom and Dad are on vacation, you don't really get much more than snores and grunts out of them before lunchtime.

"Come on, let's go out," Robyn said. I scrawled a quick note, propped it up on the kitchen table, and followed Robyn outside.

We wandered around the village, talking and looking in shop windows. We paused outside Potluck, the pottery shop owned by Robyn's friend Annie. She used to be Robyn's mom's best friend, but Robyn's mom had died just over a year ago, and Annie and Robyn's dad hadn't seen eye to eye since then. They'd made up last time we were here, though.

"How are things?" I asked nervously.

"Fine," Robyn said with a smile. "She and Dad are totally cool now. She comes over for dinner every Friday, and I'm allowed to see her whenever I want. She and Dad even go out walking together on the weekends sometimes."

"I'm so glad," I said. The shop was closed, but we stood looking at all the plates and bowls and animals in the window.

I was admiring a particularly handsome dragon when suddenly someone barged into me out of nowhere, knocking me forward so hard, I almost bumped into the window.

"Hey!" I spun around and came face-to-face with a woman staring into my eyes in a way that really creeped me out. She was hunched over, with an enormous multicolored shawl looped over her shoulders and over the top of her head, a tiny little face that you could hardly see because the shawl was spread halfway across it, and a pair of beady bright green eyes boring straight into mine.

"Sorry," I said automatically, and then felt foolish. Someone barges into me, almost bashes my nose against a shop window, and I apologize to them!

The woman stared into my eyes for another moment. Then, wrapping her shawl more firmly over her shoulders, she glanced around. She seemed to see something in the distance, because she suddenly shook herself and began to turn away. "Look after your mother!" she said in a rasping voice.

"What?" I said. "Why? My mother looks after *me*!"

But the woman was already walking away. A dark storm cloud seemed to follow her down the street. "Just do it!" she called over her shoulder.

A moment later, the cloud had turned to rain, fat heavy drops plopping down on the pavement all the way up the street. As the woman scurried away and out of sight, Robyn and I hunched together in the shop doorway and waited for the rain to stop.

"Well, that was bizarre," Robyn said.

"Wasn't it?"

"Did you see the way she stared at you?" Robyn threw her coat over the top of her head, wrapping it around her face just like the woman's shawl. "I'm a strange little lady in a very weird outfit," she said, imitating the woman's rasping voice. "And you must do as I say!"

Then she laughed and pulled at my arm. "Come on," she said as the rain shower passed. "Let's head back."

I followed her, lost in my thoughts. I'd laughed at Robyn's impression, but there was something about the woman. Something about the way she'd looked at me. Her eyes. I couldn't get them out of my mind. They reminded me of something, but I couldn't think what it was.

I shook myself as we headed to the back of the shop and poured a couple of glasses of juice. I was being silly—my imagination working overtime as usual.

By the time we went upstairs to Robyn's room with our drinks and some magazines from the shop, I'd forgotten all about the weird woman.

*　　*　　*

"Want to play a computer game?" Robyn asked.

I looked up from my magazine to see her opening a bag from the side of her desk. "I didn't know you had your own computer," I said. Robyn had e-mailed me lots of times in the last few months, but she'd always used her dad's computer downstairs in the shop.

"Annie just gave it to me for Christmas. It's her old one." She pulled a laptop out of the bag and opened it up on her desk. "It's pretty old, but it works well enough. Come on, I'll show you a new site I found."

I squeezed onto the seat with her and waited while the screen booted up. Before long, we were having ketchup-bottle gunfights, bursting balloons over each other's castles, and chasing each other around virtual mazes.

I scanned the site's list for a game we hadn't played yet. As I looked down the screen, something caught my eye. "What's that?" I asked, pointing to a tiny little star flashing in different colors around the screen. First it was orange, then it changed to yellow, then blue, flashing on and off so gently and moving around the screen so swiftly, it was hard to follow.

"What's what?"

"Wait, it's gone. You'll see it in a minute."

A moment later, it was there again, flashing at the top of the screen, so faint you would miss it if you weren't looking out for it. "That!" I said.

Robyn shook her head. "I don't know. I haven't noticed it before."

The flashing star had caught my curiosity. "Let's see what it is," I said.

We tried to trace it around the screen, while I pointed and shouted "There!" every few seconds, and Robyn chased after it with the mouse and clicked — just a second too late each time.

"It's impossible!" she said, passing the mouse to me. "Here, you try."

I tried for another minute or two with no luck. I was about to give up and suggest having another ketchup-bottle fight instead when the star appeared again. This time, I somehow managed to click at the right moment, and the star was instantly replaced by a bright white box with some squiggly text slowly coming into focus. "Got it!" I said with a smile.

"I hope we get more than a little box saying congratulations after all that effort," Robyn said.

We stared and stared at the squiggly writing, but it didn't get any clearer. It just squiggled across the box, rising and falling in sharp peaks and valleys.

"Not even that!" I said sarcastically. "Great game, I must say!" I moved the mouse over to close the box. "Come on, let's go back to —"

"Wait!" Robyn grabbed the mouse. "Look. What does it remind you of?"

I watched the lines squiggle up and down across the page a bit more. "I dunno," I said. "Maybe those charts you get in hospitals that record your heartbeat and stuff."

"Exactly. It's showing the levels of something. Hold on a sec." Robyn moved the mouse to the volume button in the corner of the screen. The volume was muted. She clicked the icon and instantly a crackling, screeching sound came through the speakers.

"Yikes — what's that?" I clapped my hands over my ears.

"I don't know! Hang on." Robyn adjusted the levels of the various audio controls, and the crackling died down to a faint hum.

"What's that one?" I asked, pointing to an icon that stood apart from the others. It looked as if it had been added on separately. The others were all square boxes with a circle inside them. This one contained a star with a red line through it.

"No idea," Robyn said.

"Try it."

She clicked the star. As she did so, the red line disappeared and the humming sound instantly stopped. The computer was silent. For about two seconds. Then something incredible happened. We heard voices coming through the speakers! And not just any voices.

"That's — that's —" Robyn stared at the screen, watching as the squiggly lines danced up and down in perfect time with the rise and fall of the two voices.

"I know!" I said, although I could hardly believe what I was hearing. "It's Daisy!"

chapter two

Daisy

"What did you think you were doing?" My supervisor's voice boomed through my MagiCell so loudly, I had to hold the phone away from my ear.

"I—I—" What could I say? I'd run out of the office so fast, I hadn't even thought of making up an excuse. Since then, all I'd focused on was trying to get a message to Philippa to warn her about her mom—which had turned out to be impossible when I couldn't appear as myself. That would be the one way to guarantee an instant image link to ATC. I didn't even want to *think* about the kind of punishment that would have meant. Interfering with another fairy's assignment is one of the worst things you can do—especially when it's not even your department!

"I'm waiting," FGRaincloud74921 said.

"I needed some air," I said feebly. "It's the office; it makes me a little claustrophobic at times."

Silence at the other end of my MagiCell. Did she believe me? Had I gotten away with it?

"How *dare* you treat me like a fool!" FGRaincloud74921 burst out so angrily, her words turned to sharp drops of rain, splattering down at me like arrows.

"I'm sorry," I said. "But I haven't really done anything I shouldn't have." In a way it was true. I'd *tried*, but I hadn't gotten anywhere. Well, how was I to know that if I became a mouse, I'd go and chew up the note I was trying to pass to Philippa? Or that she'd shrug off the old woman as a weirdo? I'd thought that somehow she'd always know it was me, no matter how I transformed. I'd even kept my own eyes both times, in case that would help.

"You are to return to ATC immediately," FGRaincloud74921 said, ignoring my plea of innocence. "We will deal with you there."

"Right," I said. "I'm on my way."

"You are close to Portal BZ 589245. Go there now. We will send someone to meet you. Do not talk to anyone, look at anyone, interact in any way with anyone or anything until you are back at ATC. Understood?"

"Totally," I said. With shaking hands, I turned off my MagiCell, let out a heavy breath, and headed for the portal.

Philippa

"You're sure it was her?" Robyn asked for about the seventh time.

"I'm positive! I'd know Daisy's voice anywhere!" Once Robyn had clicked the star and removed the crackle, the voices had come through as clearly as if they'd been in the room with us. "But I've got no idea what they were talking about."

"Me neither," Robyn agreed. We'd only heard a small slice of a conversation. Probably about ten seconds — and none of it had made sense.

"Is there any way of playing it again?" I asked.

We searched the screen. Robyn held the cursor over the bottom of the box, and a new line of controls came into view. "There!" I said. A button in the middle had an arrow on it, like the play button on a remote control. "Try that."

Robyn clicked the button — and the snatch of conversation that we'd already heard played over again. If I'd had any doubts before, I certainly didn't now. "It's *definitely* her," I said. "But what are they talking about?" The other voice was telling Daisy to go back to ATC, then reeling off a bunch of numbers and talking about something called a portal.

"I don't know," Robyn said. "But those numbers must mean something."

"It sounded like they related to the portal. But what's a portal?"

Robyn shook her head. "I don't know. There's something about the style of those numbers, though. It reminds me of something. Like a map reference, perhaps."

"Of course!" I jumped to my feet. "Have you got a pen and paper?"

Robyn pulled a drawer open. "In here."

I grabbed a pen and opened up a spiral notebook. "OK, play it again," I said.

Robyn hit the play button and the conversation started over again. When it got to the numbers, I scribbled down exactly what I heard.

"Come on," I said, tearing the page off the pad.

"Where are we going?" Robyn asked, getting up from her seat.

"Downstairs to the shop. The map section! There must be something there that'll help us figure out what this is."

She paused. "I don't know. I mean, do you think we should? We don't know what we're messing with. I mean—this was Annie's computer. She must have been linked up to Daisy's MagiCell from her last assignment, but I bet this is all top-secret fairy stuff."

Annie's a fairy godmother herself. We only found out when I was here for fall break. She's actually a really important one. The Dream Maker—that's the fairy godmother in charge of creating and distributing dreams all around the world. That was probably why her computer had access to fairies' conversations like the one we'd heard. I was sure Robyn was right—we hadn't been meant to hear it. But at the same time, it was *Daisy's* voice we'd heard! And I knew Daisy well enough to be able to tell from the tone of her voice that something was seriously wrong.

"I can't leave Daisy to get into trouble without trying to help," I said.

Robyn nodded. "I know. You're right," she said, leading the way down to the shop. "Come on, let's see what we can find."

*   *   *

Half an hour later, we were back in Robyn's bedroom with a pile of maps and guidebooks. We'd looked up the word *portal* while we were in the shop and found it was a kind of doorway. So Daisy had been told to go to a fairy doorway!

We'd narrowed the numbers down to some sort of map coordinates but hadn't figured out whether it was some kind of GPS thing or what. I sat by the radiator, leafing through an atlas.

Then Robyn picked up a map from the pile we hadn't looked at yet. "Philippa — look!"

I put the atlas down and looked to see what she was holding. It was a local map, with the words *Chiverton Maps: JK & BZ* on the cover.

I looked at the letters I'd written down. "BZ," I said. "Do you think it's in here?"

Robyn started unfolding the map. "Only one way to find out."

We spread the map across the bed. "If I remember from geography, the first three numbers are along the bottom and the second three go up the side," Robyn said. She ran a finger along the bottom line and another up the side of the map. They met at a point roughly in the center of the map. "That's where it is," she said. "Somewhere around this point."

We scoured the map, looking for anything in the area that could possibly be a fairy doorway.

"That's it — it must be!" Robyn cried, suddenly jabbing a finger at a symbol right in the middle of where we were looking.

I checked the symbol against the key on the back. "Archaeological site?"

"It's Tidehill Rocks!" Robyn said excitedly.

"Tidehill Rocks?" I repeated. "Isn't that —"

"Yes!" Robyn gathered up the map and started putting her shoes on. "The stone circle. It has to be there. Tidehill Rocks must be a fairy portal!"

We clambered up the hill, squelching through mud and wiping rain off our faces. We followed the path that led from the main road all the way up into the woods, even scrambling up a sheer hillside where the ground had collapsed earlier.

"Be careful," Robyn said. "There was a landslide here last year when there was lots of flooding. You'll be OK as long as you don't go off the path — the edge is a lot closer than you think. Follow me."

I had no intention of going off the path. I couldn't see far beyond it anyway, through the damp mist that was settling more and more heavily around us as we walked farther into the forest. I followed her steadfastly until the ground evened out again and we could walk side by side. In the distance, a startling sight came into view.

"Wow," I said, stopping to wipe another strand of wet hair out of my eyes.

"I know," Robyn said. "Amazing, aren't they? There's nothing like coming over this hill and seeing them."

Tidehill Rocks stood ahead of us: a circle of large stones, standing proud and majestic and solitary, a line of mist hovering around them, like a band holding them together. As we drew closer, I could see there were nine stones making up the circle, and a larger one probably four or five times my height in the center.

"They're incredible," I whispered, so awed by the sight, I didn't want to speak too loudly. A feeling of peace spread through me as we drew closer. This place felt magical. Nothing bad could happen here!

There were a couple of other people there — a man walked his dog, and a woman wrapped up in a big coat walked around the stones while she talked on a cell phone. A stab of irritation ran through me. Imagine coming to a place as beautiful and sacred as this and talking on your phone!

We looked everywhere. Daisy wasn't there.

"How long should we wait?" Robyn asked.

"I have no idea," I said. "Maybe she's already left. Maybe she's not here yet. Let's hang around a bit."

Robyn nodded, and we kept on wandering around the stones. The woman was on the other side, still talking on her cell phone. The man with the dog eventually left.

I couldn't stop staring at the stones. They were so big, and they'd been there for thousands of years, and yet no one had any idea who'd put them there, or why. I guess that was part of what made them feel so special — the mystery of it.

Robyn suddenly grabbed me. "Philippa!" She pulled me down behind a stone and pointed at the woman on the other side of the rocks.

"What?"

"That woman. I just caught a glimpse of her face."

"And?"

"It's the same woman who bumped into you earlier."

I crouched down behind the stone next to Robyn. The last thing we needed now was to get into a conversation with a weird person who was going to bark strange orders at me. "Let's wait here till she's gone," I said.

The woman hadn't seen us, and I couldn't hear what she was saying on her phone — the wind was carrying her words in the opposite direction — but every now and then I caught a glimpse of her face and she looked anguished. There was something about her eyes. . . . What *was* it?

"Hey, look!" Robyn pulled me away from my thoughts. She was scratching away at the stone in front of where we were crouched. Just above the ground, there was something engraved into the stone.

"What does it say?"

Robyn rubbed away at the moss and mud around the words. "I don't know. Help me."

We worked together to wipe the muck out of the letters. "I guess not many people crouch down behind the stones," I said.

"I bet we're the first people to see this for hundreds of years!" Robyn's eyes were sparkling with excitement. I wasn't so thrilled, to be honest. We were here to find Daisy, and I was pretty sure once we'd rubbed the dirt out of the words, it would just be an old signature. A twelfth-century version of *Jill was here* or something.

It was hard to make out at first — the writing was old-fashioned, and the engraving was quite faint. But once we'd cleared away the dirt, we could read it. It was a poem. Robyn read it aloud.

> *Follow a fairy 'round the stones,*
> *Amongst a hundred trees.*
> *Call her name and catch her eye,*
> *And join her world with ease.*

I stared at the poem, my jaw so wide open it began to ache. "Fairies," I managed to say eventually.

Robyn was equally stunned. "We were right. This really is a fairy portal!" she said.

"So you think the poem is for real, not just someone messing around?"

"Why would they write it way down here, virtually out of sight at the bottom of a stone, if they were messing around? And look how old-fashioned the writing is."

"Wow," I said lamely as I read the poem again. What did it mean? What *could* it mean?

Just then a sound broke into my thoughts. The woman on her phone. She was close enough for us to hear her now. I almost wanted to jump out and shout at her: "How can you wander around here talking on your stupid phone when this place is so magical?" But I didn't, of course. For two main reasons. The first reason was that I'm not the kind of person who does that sort of thing. And the second reason — well, the second reason was only just starting to dawn on me.

"Robyn!" I whispered, grabbing her arm. "Listen!"

"That woman?" she asked. "I know; how dare she —"

"No! What she was saying—did you hear her?"

By then, she'd walked by and was heading away from us again, and she'd put her phone away in her pocket. But the snippet of conversation I'd overheard was enough to convince me that I was right. I didn't hear the whole thing, but I was sure I'd heard her say something that humans generally don't know anything about.

Robyn shook her head.

"I only heard a few seconds, but I'm positive about what I heard."

"What? What did you hear? What did she say?"

I paused. Was I imagining it? Did I just *want* it to be true? Would Robyn laugh at me if I told her? No—none of those things mattered. I knew what I'd heard, and suddenly I knew what I had to do. "She said, 'See you at ATC.' I'm sure of it," I said, getting up from behind the stone and brushing my legs off. "Wait here; I'm going to check it out."

Then I followed the woman as she walked around the stones. She still hadn't turned around. Still hadn't noticed me. I held my breath as I followed her, passing one stone after another, until we reached the last one. *Follow a fairy 'round the stones, amongst a hundred trees. . . .*

And then we passed the final stone. *Call her name and catch her eye, and join her world with ease.*

Taking a deep breath, and praying I didn't have this wrong and was about to make the biggest idiot of myself, I stood still and called out as loudly as I could, "Daisy!"

For a moment, nothing happened. My cheeks burned. I'd made a fool of myself. I was wrong. Robyn *would* laugh at me.

And then the woman turned around, looking to see who had spoken, her face crinkled up in confusion and disbelief. And then she saw me. Looking me straight in the eyes, she grinned so widely that I was left in no doubt at all.

"Philippa!" she shouted. And in that moment, everything disappeared. The ground, the stones, Robyn — everything except me and Daisy. She was no longer the weird woman; she had transformed into the Daisy I knew. Her blond curly hair, her smile, her sharp green eyes — the eyes that I suddenly realized I'd recognized in the woman, that had troubled me so much when I couldn't figure out why I knew them. They were Daisy's eyes!

For a moment, I thought I was fainting. The feeling reminded me of the one time I'd gone on the

Tilt-A-Whirl at a fair — sick and dizzy from spinning around and around, feeling as if the ground was falling away from me.

I shut my eyes, hoping that would make the feeling go away. But when I opened them again, they only confirmed that this wasn't the temporary feeling of dizziness you get from a carnival ride. The ground really *was* falling away from me!

I looked around and all I could see was Daisy, spinning and hovering above the world beside me as we both rose higher and higher into the huge, great, black nothingness of space.

chapter three

Robyn

I walked around the stones in a daze. "Philippa?"
I called out to the empty sapce where she'd been
standing a moment ago. What had happened to
her? How had she disappeared like that? It was
impossible — but it had definitely happened. Philippa
and that weird woman had disappeared, right in
front of my eyes!

What had Philippa shouted? I'd seen her follow
the woman and heard her shout something, but I
couldn't hear what it was. I'd heard the woman's
reply, though. She'd called Philippa's name! How
did she know her? Who *was* she?

A thought was starting to form in my head. I bent down behind the stone to read the poem again. *Follow a fairy 'round the stones, amongst a hundred trees. Call her name and catch her eye, and join her world with ease.*

Was it possible? Could the weird woman have been a fairy? Could she even have been . . .

No. It was ridiculous. Impossible!

But the more I thought about it, the stronger my conviction became. It was the only answer that made sense. Not that it actually *did* make sense. Not the kind of sense that most people would understand, anyway.

But it was the only explanation that fit. Philippa had been trying to tell me something about the woman. Something she'd just figured out.

And we already knew that Daisy was meant to be meeting someone at the stones. However impossible, I was more and more convinced it was true: the weird woman was Daisy!

Which just left one question: *what had happened to them both?*

Philippa

"Philippa, take my hand. Hold on to me!"

Daisy was calling to me across the blackness. "It's OK," she said as I reached out to her. "It'll pass soon. Just hold on another minute."

I shut my eyes and concentrated all my efforts into trying not to be sick. "Please stop now," I whispered under my breath. "Please make the spinning feeling go away."

And then it did. Just as Daisy had said it would.

I opened my eyes and looked around me. We were in a corridor that seemed to stretch on and on as far as I could see. All around me were bright white walls, long and clean and clinical, like a hospital. Daisy was beside me.

"Is it really you?" I asked.

Daisy smiled. "Of course it is!" she said. Then she threw her arms around me in a happy hug. "How did you *find* me? And how have you managed to follow me here?"

"I'm not really sure!" I said. "We heard something on Robyn's computer and it sounded like you, so we went up to the stones and —" My words were coming out in a jumble. Everything was suddenly so confusing. "Oh, Daisy — I have no idea how this happened, really!" I confessed. "But I'm so happy to see you! I've really missed you!"

"Me, too." But she wasn't smiling anymore. She suddenly looked as serious as I'd ever seen her.

"Daisy, what is it?" I asked. "What's wrong?"

"I've been trying to contact you for days," she said.

"I know. I didn't realize at the time. But then it clicked at the stone circle—you were that odd woman, weren't you?"

"Among other things."

"Other things?" Then I made another connection. The green eyes! "Daisy, were you the mouse as well?"

She nodded.

"I'm sorry. I didn't know! I just didn't expect it."

Daisy waved a hand. "It's fine. Listen, I have to tell you something. It's really important—but I'm not supposed to tell you. I could get into *serious* trouble."

"What is it?" I asked, a knot of anxiety starting to form in my stomach.

Daisy opened her mouth to reply, but just then, something beeped in her pocket.

"Hang on." She pulled out her MagiCell—that's a fairy's electronic device, which gives her all the information she needs for her assignments and keeps her in touch with ATC. Then I realized, of course! The funny woman — Daisy — hadn't been talking on a cell phone at the stone circle; she'd been talking to someone from ATC on her MagiCell.

"I understand," Daisy was saying. "Yes, of course. Yes, I will. Immediately." Then she clicked off her MagiCell and put it back in her pocket. "I've got to go — now," she said to me. Her face had turned pale.

"What is it?" I asked.

Daisy shook her head. "I have to get back, before I'm in even more trouble."

"Back where? What kind of trouble? Daisy, what's going on?"

"Come on," she said tightly. "I'll explain everything on the way."

And with that, she turned and led the way down the bright, white, never-ending corridor.

"I'll start at the beginning," Daisy said as we walked briskly along the corridor. "I've been working in a new department since I finished my last assignment. It's called ALD — Admin and Liaison Department. My job is to match fairies with clients. And that's all I'm allowed to do. Not get involved or interfere in any way. That's *strictly* against the Fairy Godmother Code."

"OK," I said, trying to take in what she was saying. I mean, I know I've had Daisy in my life for a while now, and I know she's a fairy godsister and all that — but it still felt amazing to hear her casually talk about fairy godmothers and their jobs and clients and things.

Daisy turned to look at me as she walked. "And then while I was working I saw a name that I recognized," she went on. The look in her eyes turned me cold inside. "It was your mom, Philippa."

"OK," I said, a little less confidently this time.

"And I wouldn't normally worry too much," she went on. "I mean, people get fairy godmother assignments for lots of reasons. It might not have been serious."

"But it was?" I asked, the anxious feeling spreading into my throat.

Daisy nodded. "Your mom's down for a fairy from the SRB department," she said solemnly.

"SRB?" I asked. "What is that?"

Daisy stopped walking and looked me in the eyes. "Something Really Bad," she said. "It's when a fairy godmother steps in to help when something really bad happens to someone."

"So they stop it from happening?" I asked hopefully.

Daisy pursed her lips and turned to continue walking. "Not exactly."

"Not exactly? What do you mean? What does SRB do, then?"

"It's complicated," she said. "And it varies. *Sometimes* the bad thing can be prevented. Sometimes there's nothing you can do. If it's meant to happen, it's meant to happen."

"Like fate?"

Daisy grimaced. "You can call it that if you like. It's dealt with by the MTB department."

"MTB?"

"Meant to Be," Daisy replied. "That's who figures out if it's something we have to let happen, or something we have to try and prevent. If they decide it's meant to be, the human will get someone from SRB to help them deal with it."

"What happens to the others?" I asked.

"They get a fairy from S&C." She glanced at me before adding, "That's Stop and Change. They are really high-level fairy godmothers. You don't mess with them."

My head was starting to swim from all the information. "So my mom was supposed to get a fairy from SRB to help her deal with something bad that was going to happen to her," I said. "But you wanted to warn me, so we could stop it from happening?"

"Correct."

"But whatever the bad thing is, it's meant to happen, and not meant to be stopped?"

"That's it exactly."

"Which means that you're not only breaking one of the most important rules of the Fairy Godmother Code, you're also meddling with some of the most powerful fairies at ATC."

Daisy nodded. "That's about the long and short of it, yes."

I let out a breath. "OK, now I see why you're looking so nervous."

We fell silent for a moment, each wrapped up in our own thoughts as we walked.

Then something occurred to me. "Daisy, what was it—the SRB? What's going to happen to my mom?"

"That's just it," Daisy said. "The file doesn't say."

My throat felt like it was full of sharp icicles. "At least you tried," I said, desperately trying to think of something positive to say. She sounded as wretched as I felt. "I know how much you wanted to help."

"I'm not giving up, Philippa. I'm not going to let something terrible happen to your mom. We'll work something out — no matter what ATC does to me." She let out a heavy sigh. "Even though now on top of whatever punishment I'm going to get, you're somehow stuck up here, and I have no idea how to get you back!"

"Daisy," I said, suddenly realizing there was something I still didn't understand.

She looked at me.

"What do you mean by 'up here'? Where are we?" I asked, half of my brain knowing what she was going to say and the other half knowing I couldn't be right. It was impossible!

Daisy met my eyes. "We're Above the Clouds," she said. "Philippa, you're at ATC!"

We turned a corner, and the corridor opened out into a large circular room. Above us, an enormous domed ceiling of colored glass sprinkled rainbows over the walls and floor. Around us, doors led off in every direction. We walked over to one on the opposite side and Daisy took her MagiCell out of her pocket.

"I'll do the talking," she said as she held her MagiCell against a panel in the middle of the door. "Whatever happens, we can't let them know you're a human, OK?"

"Surely they'll be able to tell! I haven't got wings!"

Daisy laughed. "You don't need them up here. Most fairies look just like you and me when they're at ATC. Look—haven't you noticed I'm the same Daisy you see on Earth?" She spun around. "No wings!"

"But don't you fly around and do . . . fairylike things up here?" I asked, feeling stupid, like someone who's just arrived somewhere for the first time where everyone else knows how it works except them. That's exactly what I was!

"Of course we do," Daisy replied. "But you can do that anyway. This is ATC. You can do virtually anything you like up here—if you know how."

"How do you fly, then?"

Daisy shrugged. "I don't know," she said. "You just kind of know that you can do it — and then you can!"

She made it sound easy, and I'm sure it was — for a fairy!

Daisy pressed a few buttons on the door. A moment later, it slowly swung open.

"Remember, act like a fairy, OK?" Daisy whispered. "Humans at ATC are *strictly* against Fairy Godmother Code. We don't want to get into even *more* trouble than we're already in."

I nodded — even though all I could think was: *how the heck do I act like a fairy?*

"Afternoon, afternoon — hi there. Hey, how are you?"

Daisy was all smiles as we walked through her office. At first glance it looked like any other kind of office. Lots of people busy bustling around, sitting at desks in front of their screens, making calls.

The only difference was — well, for one thing, there was no floor below us. Secondly, things kept appearing out of nowhere.

"How do they do that?" I asked as we walked past a fairy sitting at a desk tapping away at her computer and reaching out to drink tea from a cup that materialized out of thin air in front of her.

"It's like everything here. You think it—it happens."

I didn't have time to wonder about it for too long, because Daisy suddenly elbowed me in the ribs. "That's my supervisor."

At the far end of the room, a small woman was walking through a door that hadn't existed a moment ago. As it closed behind her it promptly disappeared again, and she looked around the room. Her eyes fell on the fairies before her; each one quickly looked up and smiled, then got straight back to his or her work. She responded with a sharp nod and walked briskly down the aisle that ran along the center of the room. Well, the *sort of* aisle. Like everything else, it didn't have a floor. I concentrated on not looking down. When I did, my insides seemed to slip away down into the nothingness below.

She seemed to hold the whole room in her power, even though she was quite small. She was probably only a little taller than me, with a very round, small face, pinched-in cheeks, gray hair cut short and neat. She wore a cotton suit with the jacket buttoned all the way up to her neck and huge gold bangles on both wrists that jangled as she made her way toward us.

As she reached us, I heard Daisy take a sharp breath. "Good afternoon, FGRaincl—"

"Come with me," the woman said tightly. She was about to turn on her heel when she spotted me. "Who is this?" she asked, scornfully looking me up and down as though I'd blown in like a piece of trash off the street.

"I'm her cousin!" I burst out without thinking.

"She's new to the department!" Daisy said at the exact same moment.

The woman narrowed her eyes and turned them first on Daisy, and then on me. Without saying a word, she slowly raised one eyebrow so high it *looked* like a question mark.

"Cousin?" the woman said eventually.

Daisy forced out a heavy laugh. "That was just a little joke, FGRaincloud," she said. "She's spent a bit too much time on Earth. She likes to call everyone her cousin. Don't you . . . *Tulip*?" she asked, staring at me fiercely and quickly nodding her head behind her supervisor's back.

I flashed the woman what I hoped was a broad, relaxed smile. I think it probably looked like someone who had been asked to bare her teeth while being tortured.

"I'm sorry, Effigy Raincloud," I said, wondering why she had such a strange name but trying to say it with confidence anyway. "I should have known better than to make such a silly joke. Daisy's right. I have obviously spent *far* too much time on Earth."

Daisy's supervisor gave me a strange look, before Daisy quickly went on. "Tulip"—I guessed that was me—"is new to ALD. Her previous supervisor's just left. She asked me to look after her," she said so boldly and smoothly, I almost believed her myself.

Her supervisor gave me another look. "Right. Well, we'll see about that," she said briskly. "Now then, there's the matter of your unauthorized Earth visit."

"I know," Daisy replied. "I'm so sorry I forgot to ask, but I wanted to do some background research on my current client list—so I can work more efficiently."

Daisy's supervisor stared at her again. "Oh," she said in the same clipped way she seemed to say everything. "I see. And you can prove this, can you?"

"Oh, yes, absolutely," Daisy replied, reaching for her MagiCell. "I'll get it all printed out and show you right now. . . ."

Her supervisor waved a hand in a kind of resigned dismissal. "That won't be necessary," she said. "But don't let me catch you going off on any more research trips without getting my permission first."

"No, I won't," Daisy said, relief through her words. "I really am sorry."

Her supervisor waved a hand again. "Right, enough of that," she said. "Now, you can get back to work. You've plenty to catch up on." She looked at me. "And I want Tulip's documents please, preferably with an explanation as to why I haven't heard about the transfer."

"Yes, FGRaincloud," Daisy said. "I'll do it right away."

A moment later, her supervisor had turned and disappeared back down the aisle. At the end of the room, she clicked her fingers and a door once again appeared out of nowhere. She opened the door, walked through it, closed it behind her, and was gone.

"How did she do *that*?" I asked, staring into the blankness that had been a door seconds earlier.

"What?" Daisy asked.

"That thing with the door."

"What thing?"

"*What thing?*" I repeated incredulously. "The door — it wasn't there, and then it was, and now it's gone again!"

Daisy shrugged. "That's how things work up here," she said. "You don't think too hard about things like that; you just do them."

"But how? I mean, could *I* do them too?"

Daisy pointed at the space below us, the nothingness we were hovering above. "It's like that," she said. "You're not thinking about it; you're just doing it. It's easy!"

I looked down, took in the huge complete emptiness underneath me — and promised myself I *definitely* wouldn't think about it.

"I'd say you got off quite lightly there," I said to change the subject.

"I know! I can't believe it. FGRaincloud must have other things on her mind. She often does, which is a good thing. She comes across as totally efficient, but luckily she's the complete opposite. As long as there's something more important preoccupying her, she usually forgets why she's even mad at you!"

"So — what are we going to do about my documents?" I asked.

Daisy shook her head. "We should get away with it for now. She's moved on to the next thing and will forget about us for a day or so. We'll easily have time to figure out how to get you back to Earth by the time she remembers about that."

"Oh, well that's good," I said, not sure I meant it. I mean, of course I wanted to get back to Earth. I didn't want to be stuck up here forever. But — well, I wouldn't mind spending a *bit* of time here. I was at ATC! I was actually in the middle of Fairy Godmother headquarters!

Except that I couldn't enjoy it. Not when my mom was in trouble. Somehow we had to try to get more details about the really bad thing that was going to happen to her. We had to *stop* it!

"Come on," Daisy said, breaking into my thoughts and knowing exactly what I was thinking. "Let's get to my desk. We've got work to do."

We sat in front of Daisy's computer. The computer looked similar to our computer at home. The weird thing was how you got it to work. You had to speak to it, and it would respond with pictures and patterns and lines and lines of text.

Daisy said that if you really knew what you were doing, you just had to *think* about what you wanted to know and it would come up with answers. I still hadn't quite gotten my head around this whole think-it-can-happen-and-hey-presto-it-*can*-happen idea yet, so I stuck to saying things out loud.

"Where am I?" I asked, just for fun.

The screen burst into light, a thousand colors spilling across it, spreading and weaving into every space in swirling, dancing loops and lines. Through the colors, three big letters emerged: ATC.

OK, I knew that.

"Who am I?" I asked. The screen went blank.

I turned to Daisy, trying not to be too freaked out. Did I still exist, or, now that I was at ATC, had I been wiped off the face of the earth forever, with no way back?

Daisy glanced at the screen. "That's good," she said.

"What? How can it be good?"

"It can only tell you what's already in its program. It's not programmed to recognize humans up here. If it doesn't know you, that means it's unlikely anyone realizes there's a human up here — yet."

"Yet?"

Daisy paused. "Well, it will catch on eventually," she said. "Any changes in the atmosphere gradually seep through and need to be identified and categorized."

Changes in the atmosphere? Identified? Categorized? "Daisy, you haven't actually made me feel a whole lot better."

"Look, trust me," she said. "If the computer doesn't know who you are, all it means is that we've got longer to plan a way of getting you out of here before we land ourselves in any more trouble."

"OK," I said.

"Good. Now, let me think. We need to find out what's happening with your mom first, and worry about the rest later."

Daisy was right. That was all that mattered right now. Finding out what was going to happen to Mom — and figuring out how we could stop it.

Daisy shut her eyes and sat in silence for a moment. The computer seemed to be waiting. I waited, too. What was she thinking? Was she asking the computer a question? Would it know the answer this time?

I looked at the screen. A small word was emerging in the center of the screen.

YES.

I stared at the word. Yes? Yes what?

YES, I WILL KNOW THE ANSWER THIS TIME.

Whoa! The computer had heard my thoughts! It was answering me!

Daisy gave me a quick nudge. "Stop thinking things," she said. "Your thoughts are getting in the way."

Stop thinking things? How was I supposed to do that?

JUST DO IT, the computer replied.

OK, this was getting spooky now. I had to stop thinking. I tried to do something Mom had once taught me when she came back from a meditation and yoga weekend. You imagine that your mind is like the sky, and if any thoughts come into it, you think of them as clouds floating slowly across it. Mom had spent a week doing it every day until she decided that she needed to spend *more* time thinking, not less. She thought it might make her brain lazy.

I shut my eyes and concentrated on the image for a while, and it must have worked, because when I opened them again, something was happening on the screen. Daisy was staring straight at it, as if she were looking into its eyes, holding a conversation with it. In reply, pictures were forming on the screen.

They were quite blurry to begin with, but then they became sharper and clearer — and as they did so, I gasped and clapped a hand over my mouth. It was the cottage my family and I were staying in! The computer was showing a series of pictures: the garden, the kitchen . . . my mom and dad!

"Daisy — look!" I cried out.

"I know. That means the SRB will happen soon. The computer only gets images when the event is imminent."

I shuddered. Something really bad was about to happen to my mom — and all we could do was watch it take place on a screen?

"Wait," Daisy said. "Let's see if we can get some volume on this and hear what's happening."

She touched the screen, and instantly I heard my mom's voice coming through the computer!

"I don't care *who* she's with," she was saying. "Or how long they've lived here. She's *my* daughter and I'm *not* happy!"

Her daughter — they were talking about me! Why was she unhappy with me?

I leaned closer to the screen.

"I know, darling," my dad replied. "I'm only saying we should give them a bit more time. Robyn knows the area like the —"

"I don't care *how* well she knows the area. You heard Martin. Even her father doesn't know where they are. They've been gone for hours, and it's getting really dark. I'm just not —"

Mom broke off as her phone rang. She practically threw herself across the table to grab it. "It's Martin," she said, checking the screen on her phone. "They must be back."

Mom answered her phone. "Martin," she said, her voice thick with relief. But as she listened, her face turned gray. "I see," she said. "Right," she added a moment later. Finally, she said, "OK, yes, if you don't mind, put Robyn on."

While she waited for Robyn to come on the phone, she turned to Dad.

"They're back, then?" Dad said, smiling at Mom. But not his usual smile, the one he wears nearly all the time because he's as happy and carefree as a baby and nothing in his world could make him do anything *other* than smile. This was more like the smile a scary clown wears — the type that's painted on to hide the unhappiness underneath it.

Mom shook her head. "Robyn's back," she said, her voice almost cracking. "Philippa's missing."

Dad slumped into a chair as though someone had punched the life out of him. Mom turned back to her phone. "Robyn," she said tightly. "Tell me what happened."

Daisy had opened a new page on her computer and was looking through a long list. She ran her finger down the list, then stopped and shook her head. "I don't believe it," she said, talking more to herself than to me. "I'm so stupid!"

"What?" I asked flatly.

"The SRB," she said, looking up as though she'd just remembered I was there. "It could be any moment now. It must have to do with your disappearance."

"Mom's SRB is my disappearance?"

Daisy shook her head. "I don't know. It's not that simple. There could be something else — maybe a *result* of your disappearance."

"But how is that possible? I only disappeared because I was coming to find you, and you already knew that something really bad was going to happen to my mom."

"I know."

"But surely that's impossible — isn't it?"

Daisy let out a long breath. "Not impossible. Just hard to understand if you're not used to the way these things work."

"Try me," I said.

"It's complicated," she admitted. "It has to do with MTB's role."

"MTB — that's the department that decides if something's meant to be?"

"That's right. The thing is, MTB is a pretty efficient team, and sometimes if they don't have a huge load of cases, they can get information on an SRB before it actually happens."

"OK," I said, half of my brain understanding what she was saying and the other half screaming at me that it couldn't possibly be true.

"Listen, Philippa," Daisy said urgently. "None of this really matters. The important thing is what's happening or going to happen to your mom."

"I know," I said, swallowing hard. "What are we going to do?"

"That's just it," Daisy said darkly. "There's nothing we *can* do now. It seems like the SRB is already in motion."

chapter four

Robyn

I held the phone to my ear with both hands, trying to stop them from shaking. "Mrs. Fisher," I began. "I'm really, really sorry."

She didn't let me get any further. "Where is she?" she burst out. "What's happened to my girl?"

"I — I —" What on earth could I say? I'd gone over it a hundred times in my head, trying to figure out what *had* happened. One minute, Philippa was there, crouched down next to me behind the stone. Then she'd gotten up and wandered around the stone circle, following the woman who we'd been hiding from. They'd both called out to each other, and then disappeared into thin air!

I couldn't make any sense of it. Except for the thought that kept niggling at the back of my mind. The thought that the weird woman was Daisy in disguise.

Could it *really* be true? And even if it was, how could I ever say anything to —

"Robyn." Mrs. Fisher's voice broke into my thoughts. "I'm not blaming you," she said tightly. "You're not in any trouble. I just want to know where my daughter is."

What could I say? *Well, you see. It's like this: Philippa disappeared into thin air, and so did this weird woman who's been following us around and whispering strange things to us. And I have a strong suspicion that actually, the weird woman wasn't really a weird woman at all, but a fairy in disguise, who is, incidentally, your daughter's other best friend.*

I don't think so.

"Mrs. Fisher, I really don't know what happened," I said. "We were at the stone circle, just hanging out, you know. And she — well, I wasn't really looking and I think she must have wandered off." This was sounding terrible! How was the idea of her daughter wandering off on her own into the forest going to make her feel better?

"The stone circle?" Mrs. Fisher said, her voice now sounding as if she were trying to speak while having her throat twisted into knots. "Tidehill Rocks? That's where you last saw her?"

"Well, yes, I guess so," I said.

"Right," Mrs. Fisher said. "Thank you, Robyn. Thank you."

A second later, I heard a click, and then the line went dead. I handed the phone back to Dad.

Dad put an arm around me. "You OK? You want to talk about this?" he asked.

I hesitated. Could I tell Dad what had happened? Would *he* believe me? I didn't dare risk it. Not when we'd been doing so well lately. For nearly a year after Mom died, he'd been like a stranger. But since everything had come out in the open, about how Mom had been a fairy and all the dreams she'd left for me and everything—well, he'd been almost back to his old self. But he had hated fairies and everything to do with them for so long that I wasn't sure it was a good idea to bring it all up again. I didn't want to spoil it by sharing half-formed thoughts about fairies and disappearances and all sorts of other things that didn't make any sense.

"Dad, can I go and look for her?" I asked.

"I'll come with you."

"No," I said quickly. "Look, I know where she was last. I'm *sure* I'll be able to find her again. Please let me go out. You stay here in case she turns up. I'll be right back." And before he had time to answer, I'd thrown a coat on, run down the stairs, and shut the shop door behind me.

Philippa

I sat, paralyzed, listening to the whole conversation between Robyn and my mom. It was awful.

I wanted to scream at the computer screen: *I'm OK, I'm OK!* But even if I could have done that without attracting the attention of an office full of fairy godmothers, it wouldn't have made any difference. They wouldn't have been able to hear me.

The screen went blank as soon as the phone call ended. "Why's it stopped?" I asked.

"I timed it for two minutes," Daisy said. "Any more than that is too risky."

"What d'you mean?"

"Those pictures were only for SRB to see. They have access to relevant scenes — people, places, conversations, anything that can help them do their job."

"So it's only SRB who should have been able to watch what we've just seen with Mom and Robyn?"

"Exactly. Breaking into their work like this is one of the easiest ways to get caught. A couple of minutes will usually go unnoticed but any more than that and they could trace us."

"Could we at least try watching Robyn?" I asked.

Daisy shook her head. "It's too risky."

"Please! Just a few seconds."

Daisy bit her lip and looked around. "Right, OK, I'll see what I can do. I may still have some access to her from my last assignment."

She shut her eyes and faced the screen. Nothing happened.

"It's not working," I said.

"Wait. Give it a chance."

I stared and stared at the blank screen. A moment later, something started to happen. A picture was forming — blurry around the edges, but I could see two people. It was Robyn and her dad!

Robyn was talking. Her voice was as faint as the picture, so it was hard to tell what she was saying. But I caught a couple of snatches of their conversation.

"Where she was last," I heard. "I'll be able to find her again. Let me go out. . . . I'll be right back."

And then the picture disappeared.

"What happened?" I asked.

"That's all I could get, and even that was more of a risk than we should be taking."

"So what do we do now?"

"I don't know," Daisy said. "Let me think a minute."

She glanced around the office, then lowered her voice. "There's only one way." She took out her MagiCell and pressed a few buttons.

As it whirred into action, I hunched down in my seat and leaned in closer. I lowered my voice, too. "What are you doing?" I asked in a whisper.

"Hacking into SRB. I'm going to try to find the exact time when the assignment is due to start. If it's tomorrow, at least we'll have the night to think it through."

A moment later, Daisy's MagiCell bleeped and flashed with a bunch of numbers and signs. Daisy

pressed a few more buttons. Then she stared at the small screen. And then she slumped in her chair.

"I'm guessing it's tonight, then," I said.

Daisy nodded.

"Did the MagiCell show anything else?"

Daisy looked away.

"Daisy, tell me. I need to know."

She turned toward me but wouldn't meet my eyes. "The team is getting ready to go," she said. "And they're dressed as an ambulance crew. They've got stretchers and everything."

I fell back in my seat, almost as though I'd been hit. Stretchers. For my mom?

"Your mom's already gone looking for you, and I think she's going to have some kind of accident on the way."

I sat in silence for a moment. My mom was going to have a terrible accident — and it was all my fault. No! I wouldn't let it happen — I *couldn't!* Come on, think. *Think!*

If Mom had already left the house, it was too late to stop her from going.

And since Robyn had told her I'd gone missing at the stone circle, I figured that's where she would be headed. But she'd never been there before, and it would be completely dark soon. She'd *never* find her way.

Then I remembered something. The path on the way to the stone circle. The flood last year. The place where if you went off the path, the ground became a sheer cliff. Mom would have to take the same path! It was the main one up from the road. But she wouldn't know about the floods or the landslide!

I didn't need a computer to tell me what was going to happen. I knew it as firmly as if Daisy's supervisor had stood in front of me and confirmed it herself.

"We have to get in touch with Robyn," I said. "We have to get her to find Mom and stop her from going up to Tidehill Rocks."

"Got it!" she said. She turned back to the computer. "Open the communication box," she said out loud. The computer sprang to life as Daisy sat looking at it, thinking so fiercely I could almost see her thoughts myself.

Of course! It was the same panel that had opened up on Robyn's computer when we'd heard Daisy's conversation with her supervisor. So perhaps we could use it to communicate with Robyn! Why hadn't we thought of this before?

A moment later, the box was open. "Come on, come on," Daisy murmured, staring at the blank box, waiting for it to find Robyn via Annie's, and now Robyn's, computer. Anticipation danced inside my stomach.

But the anticipation soon began to flutter and die. The connection didn't go through. Nobody was there. Robyn must have already left. Every second seemed to last an hour, each one passing in useless, awful silence.

And every second that passed was another one wasted, and another one closer to the moment when Mom would have a terrible accident — all because of me.

"I can't bear it," I said. "I feel so useless."

"Me, too." Daisy was fidgeting and glancing around.

"What is it?" I asked. "Who are you looking for?"

Daisy leaned in close again. "My supervisor," she whispered. "I have an idea."

"What?"

"Listen, take the desk next to mine. It's been empty for weeks anyway. I'm going back down there. I'm going after your mom. I'll stop her from going to the woods."

"But how? She's probably halfway there by now. And you don't even know where the dangerous part is. You'll never find her."

"Well, I'll find Robyn, then. She can show me!"

"Daisy, how will you get Robyn to listen to you? If you go down as yourself, they'll find you immediately and you'll be in the worst trouble ever. You know you can't risk that, especially now."

"You're right," she said glumly. "I probably won't even get out of the door if I go as myself."

"And if you go in disguise, she'll *never* listen to you. Look what happened with me! All the attempts you made to get me to listen to you, and I just wrote you off as a weirdo. How will you convince Robyn it's really you?"

Daisy looked as miserable as I felt. "I can't believe it," she said. "After all this, we just have to sit around and wait for something awful to happen to your mom. If only we knew how to get you down there."

And that's when it hit me.

"Daisy," I said, finally filled with real hope. "I've got it. The one thing that will ensure that Robyn will listen to you!"

"What's that?" she asked.

"You need to go now," I said, practically dragging her out of her chair. "Use the portal and go back down to Earth. Then find my mom! If you can't find her, find Robyn! Get to the dangerous place, before my mom does. Hurry!"

"But how will I get your mom to listen to me?" she asked. "She'll think I'm as crazy as you did. We've already established that she won't —"

"Daisy," I said firmly. "You'll have to go as me!"

chapter five

Daisy

I emerged from the portal and looked around. It was six o'clock and already so dark it felt like night. I clicked a couple of buttons on my MagiCell to increase my vision capability and looked around. Nothing. No one was here.

Looking down at myself, I had a really weird feeling. It didn't normally bother me—transporting as other people or as animals or whatever. But to be here as Philippa! It felt so strange. Almost as if it wasn't just a disguise, but that I had her with me, almost as if I *was* her, seeing the world through her eyes. Experiencing her feelings.

I walked away from the stones, toward the path. If I followed this, at some point I should meet Philippa's mom, or at least Robyn, coming up the path. What if I'd made a mistake and Philippa's mom wasn't going to veer off the path at all? Maybe the SRB was something else. Or perhaps I'd gotten the whole thing wrong and nothing bad was going to happen to her at all!

Except I knew better than that. I'd seen it. SRB doesn't make mistakes. Something bad was going to happen soon—unless I stopped it.

Just then, I heard a noise in the distance. A rustling of footsteps on the path—twigs breaking, mud squelching. Someone was coming toward me!

I sped up again, hurrying toward the footsteps. Rounding a corner, I saw her.

"Robyn!" I yelled in utter relief. She was here! I'd found her!

She peered in my direction through the darkness. Another few steps toward me and she saw me too. "Philippa!" Her face was one enormous beaming smile of relief. She threw her arms around me. "Oh, Philippa, I've been so worried. What happened to you? For a moment I thought you'd—well, I've been thinking all sorts of ridiculous thoughts! Come on, let's get back to your parents."

"Yes, we have to find Philippa's mom—and I think she's on her way here," I said.

Robyn laughed. "Philippa's mom?" she said. "Your mom, you mean."

I paused. How was I going to explain this? "Look," I said. "I know this is going to be hard to believe, but I'm not Philippa."

Robyn laughed again. "OK, whatever you say. I'm not Robyn either, then. Who should we be? Catwoman and Wonder Woman? Hey, yeah, that'd be fun. But can I be—"

"I'm not joking!" I said seriously.

Robyn looked at me but didn't say anything.

"It's not a game," I said. "I promise. Philippa *did* disappear. She went to ATC with me. The poem you read on the stone, about following a fairy around the stones—she followed me!"

"But—but there was just that funny woman up here with us," Robyn said. "Wasn't there?"

"Yes, it was a woman," I said. "But that was just a disguise, like this. It's so that ATC doesn't catch me and stop me from doing what I've come here to do."

"So it's, it really was—you're—" Robyn stared at me, but didn't go on.

"Robyn, it's me, Daisy," I said softly. "Philippa's still at ATC."

Robyn nodded silently.

"She'll come back soon, I promise, once we've figured out how. But I'm here because something really bad is due to happen to her mom any minute now, and we have to stop it."

Robyn's face paled. "What's going to happen?"

"I don't know. But it's going to happen very, very soon. Philippa says you might be able to lead me to the place we think she might fall. Something to do with flooding and a landslide."

In an instant, Robyn's attitude completely changed. She was in charge now. "Come on," she said. "I know where you mean. Tell me the rest on the way."

And with that, she turned and led the way, and as I followed her, I told her everything—and silently prayed we wouldn't be too late.

"Here," Robyn said after we'd walked for several minutes. We left the path, inching carefully over to the place where the hill fell sharply away to a chasm below.

"How did that happen?" I asked.

"There used to be mining caves near here, so the land was already quite unstable, and then whole chunks of it were ripped off in storms last year. That's why there are signs telling you to stay on the path."

"Signs that you can't see in the dark," I said.

"Exactly. If anything's going to happen to your mom—I mean to Philippa's mom—this is where it's likely to happen."

I looked down and peered into the darkness below us. What if she was already down there? Perhaps we were too late. We yelled down to see if anyone was there but got no response. So, I checked my MagiCell, hacking in once again to SRB's mission. I knew I was really pushing things now. Every time I did that, I was increasing the risk of being found out. But I couldn't come this far and fail now. We had to stop the accident. Nothing else mattered.

My screen bleeped. There was an SRB squad fifteen minutes away! Whatever the event was, SRB had been alerted and it was going to happen very soon! At least that meant we weren't too late. Philippa's mom wasn't lying injured—or worse—at the bottom of the chasm. We still had time!

"Robyn, you are sure this is the right place, aren't you?" I asked urgently.

"Positive," Robyn said. "There aren't any other dangers around here at all. If she's on her way up here, this is where it'll be." Then she shook her head. "I'm such an idiot," she said.

"Why?"

"Why didn't I think to say I'd go with her? I could have made sure she stuck to the path."

I touched Robyn's arm. "Hey, don't blame yourself," I said. "She was due for the SRB way before you spoke to her. There was nothing you could have done."

Robyn looked down at her feet. "OK," she said flatly. "I just feel so useless standing here. Maybe we should go looking for her?"

"You're right. Maybe we can meet her before she even gets here."

We picked our way carefully along the unstable ground, halfway between the dangerous precipice and the path. And then I saw a shape in the distance. It was her!

"Robyn," I said. "There she is!"

"Mrs. Fisher!" I called before I could stop myself. She stopped and looked around. And in that moment, searching into the darkness to see who had called to her, she stepped off the path and began to come toward us—and the precipice.

"What are we going to do?" I asked, cold panic seeping through me.

Robyn looked at me openmouthed. "Well, for one thing, you can't go around shouting 'Mrs. Fisher' when you look like Philippa!" she said.

"I know, I know. I don't know what I was thinking." I glanced up to see Philippa's mom coming closer, straight toward the edge of the precipice.

"Robyn, do something!" I screeched, pushing her forward. "I can't go. I'll never get away with pretending to be Philippa to her. She'll see through me!"

Robyn ran toward Philippa's mom. "Mrs. Fisher!" she called.

Philippa's mom spotted Robyn. "Oh, it's only you, Robyn," she said, her face full of disappointment. She kept picking her way toward the chasm at the edge of the hill.

"Don't go down there!" Robyn said. "You've gone off the path." She tried to steer Mrs. Fisher back onto the path. "Look, we need to head back this way," she said gently.

"But maybe she's down here! Maybe this is where she went!"

"It's too dangerous this way," Robyn said. "We need to get back on the path."

"But that's the whole point!" Mrs. Fisher said, pressing on determinedly. "If it's dangerous, it's even more likely that Philippa's stuck down there and that's why she hasn't come home. I have to get to her!"

"She's not down there!" Robyn shouted to Mrs. Fisher's retreating back.

"Who says she isn't? How can you be sure?" she replied without even slowing her stride. She was heading right for the edge!

And then she lost her footing and slipped on the loose ground.

No! Please, no!

Without stopping to think, I ran toward her. She was slipping and sliding down the bank toward the drop-off. I got to her seconds before she reached the edge and grabbed her coat before she fell any farther.

She turned toward me and looked directly into my eyes, her expression frozen. *She knows it's not Philippa*, I thought.

And then her face broke into the biggest smile I'd ever seen.

"Philippa!" she cried. "My darling girl. Oh, my baby. Oh, Philippa!" Scrabbling to get back up onto the path, she reached out for me. A moment later, her arms were around me, squeezing me so hard that for a few seconds I couldn't breathe. "Philippa, oh, I've been so worried; I was terrified something awful . . ." She held me away from her, looking at me, stroking my hair, smiling into my eyes, then pulling me close for another enormous hug. She was half laughing and half crying. "What happened to you?" she asked, looking into my eyes so intensely that I was convinced she must know it wasn't really Philippa. *Surely* she could see me in there.

But she didn't. She just kept on smiling at me—at Philippa—and laughing with pleasure.

"I—I'm sorry," I said, steering her back onto the path with me. "I—we were playing a game, weren't we, Robyn?"

I looked at Robyn. She glanced nervously at Philippa's mom, then back at me. "Yes!" she said. "We were. That's right, we were playing a game, and you got lost, didn't you Dais—Philippa?"

"I was hiding," I said. "We were playing hide and seek, and it was my turn to hide—but I got lost and Robyn couldn't find me, and then I couldn't find her, and I didn't know where I was. And—oh, Mom." I cleared my throat. I'd never called anyone "Mom" before. It felt weird. But it also felt—what was it? I decided to try saying it again to see if I could figure it out. "Mom, I'm really sorry," I said.

Mrs. Fisher wrapped me closer in her arms. "Oh, darling, it doesn't matter," she said, kissing my head. "All that matters is that you're safe."

That was when I realized what it felt like to say "Mom." It felt really, really, *really* nice.

She took my hand as we walked back along the path in the darkness. "Robyn, are you coming back with us?" I asked.

"I'll come over in a bit," she said. "You'll want to do a bit of catching up with—your parents."

I nodded, then smiled as Philippa's mom squeezed my hand. "OK," I said, hoping I'd be able to keep my act going without Robyn to back me up. "See you later."

The second Philippa's mom and I walked through the door, her dad came running toward us and gathered me up in an enormous bear hug.

"I'll make some hot drinks," Philippa's mom said. As she poured three hot chocolates and I helped Philippa's dad build a fire in the family room, I felt overwhelmed by a warmth I'd never, ever experienced before.

I knew it was only temporary. I even knew it wasn't real. But I knew something else, too: I liked it. I liked it a lot.

As soon as I got the chance, I checked my MagiCell. I put in the numbers for Mrs. Fisher's SRB.

Nothing. The numbers weren't recognized. The SRB had been erased!

"Yes!" I punched the air. We'd done it! We'd completely stopped it!

I wished so much that I could contact Philippa, but I didn't dare risk it. ATC would know that someone had stopped the SRB, and it wouldn't take them long to figure out that I'd disappeared again, either. I was going to be in *so* much trouble. The last thing I wanted was for ATC to link me to Philippa and get her into trouble too.

"Philippa, the hot chocolate's ready!" Mrs. Fisher called.

I'd figure out how to get us out of this soon, but I wanted to enjoy pretending to be Philippa for a *bit* longer first.

Philippa

I flew down the corridor and back to my desk.

Listen to me! *I flew down the corridor!*

I really did! Daisy had been right. All I had to do was act as if it was the most normal thing in the world and believe that I could do it without thinking about it — and I *could* do it!

Not very far, and not very high off the ground or anything. But I actually, really did fly.

I was still buzzing and excited about it when I got back to my desk, and I was desperate to tell Daisy what I'd done, but, more importantly, to hear if my mom was OK. I looked around to check that no one was watching, and then I took my new MagiCell out of my pocket. Daisy's boss had given it to me earlier. Apparently you get a new one each time you start in a new department — another thing I had to act normal about.

"Great, thanks," I said, trying to sound casual when she handed it to me.

"Well?" she said, frowning at me with tight lips.

"Um. Thank you very much?" I faltered. Was that what she wanted?

She just *tsskk*ed sharply and walked off.

The fairy at the next desk had popped her head over. She was a girl about my same age — or at least that was how she appeared to me. "I think she was expecting you to program it," she said with a smile.

"Oh, yeah, of course she was!" I said as though this was the most obvious thing in the world and it had only slipped my mind for a moment. "I'll do it now."

The girl had laughed. "Here, I'll do it for you," she said. "You probably don't know the codes."

"Codes? Why wouldn't I know them?" I'd replied quickly. Had she guessed that I was an imposter? Was it that obvious?

"Because you're new!" she said simply. Then she hopped over to my side of the divide. "I'm Tabitha," she said. "Or Tabby to my friends."

I smiled at her. "I'm . . . Tulip. I'm a new fairy godsister here."

Tabitha burst out laughing. "Fairy godsister!" she said. "I like it! I'm going to use that all the time from now on!"

I felt my face heat up with embarrassment. I was getting *everything* wrong!

She didn't seem too bothered. She punched a few buttons on my MagiCell and handed it back to me. "There you go," she said with another smile. "Ready for action!"

"Thanks," I muttered.

"No problem," she said, slipping back around to her desk. "See you in a bit. Give me a shout if you need anything."

I was conscious of her now, on the other side of the thin divide. Even if I managed to figure out how to contact Daisy on my MagiCell, what if Tabitha heard me? Would she tell on me?

But I needed to know what had happened with my mom. Had Daisy stopped the SRB? I had to find out. I *had* to know what had happened to Mom.

I looked at the MagiCell in my hand and decided to try the most obvious solution. That seemed to be the way things worked best around here.

I touched the screen and it immediately lit up, as did a picture of a keyboard. I punched in a few letters and hoped it would work: C-A-L-L-D-A-I-S-Y.

The MagiCell responded by making a soft whirring sound and scrolling through what looked like a million pages of names. Then the scrolling stopped. FG NUMBER? appeared on the screen.

FG number? Fairy Godmother number? How was I supposed to find out Daisy's Fairy Godmother number?

Her desk was next to mine. Maybe there'd be something there.

Putting on the most casual manner I could, I flew — yes, flew again! — over to Daisy's desk and casually rummaged through some files and folders that were lying around.

"Need any help?" Tabitha's face popped up over the divide again.

My face instantly reddened. She knew I was meddling! *Act normal. Act normal.*

"Oh, just looking for Daisy's FG number," I said, wishing my ears would stop feeling quite so hot.

Tabitha nodded in an understanding kind of way. "We keep them stuck inside the bottom drawer," she said, pointing to a line of light flowing underneath the desk.

I nodded back in what I hoped was an equally knowing manner. "Ah. Of course!" I said, wondering how in the world I was meant to open a line of light!

Two seconds later, Tabitha came around and did it for me. She just touched the line with her finger, and the light bounced open into ten different colors. Tabitha flicked through them till she reached the bottom one. A moment later, a line of numbers danced out of the light and into my hand. I closed my hand around them, hoping I'd be able to keep hold of them long enough to put them into my MagiCell.

"Thanks again," I said.

"No problem. I know how hard it is when you start in a new department."

"Yes, it is," I said awkwardly.

"I start in a new one myself soon," she said. Then she lowered her voice. "I'm not really meant to talk about it yet. You know, FGC Section 37421 and all that."

"Oh, yes," I said. "That old thing!"

Tabitha laughed again. "You're funny!" she said. "You're not like other fairy godmothers — or should I say fairy godsisters!"

Oh, no! She knew I wasn't one of them! "No, I am, really," I said enthusiastically. "I'm just the same. I'm *exactly* like all the other fairy godsisters. Look, see. I do this, like all the others." I flew back to my desk. "And this." I opened up my hand and let the numbers float into the air. I quickly punched them into my MagiCell before they flew off and I had no way of getting them back. "See!" I said with the brightest smile I could force onto my face. "Totally normal!"

Tabitha laughed and shook her head. "OK, if you say so."

As the MagiCell whirred away softly, searching for Daisy's FG number, Tabitha kept on talking. "It's a shame I'm going," she said. "Just when a cool new fairy godsister comes along."

A cool new fairy godsister? She meant me! For a moment, I was so taken aback, I couldn't think of anything else. Me — ordinary Philippa Fisher — she saw *me* as a cool fairy godsister! Despite everything going on with my mom and with Daisy, I couldn't suppress a smile.

"When do you go?" I asked.

"Couple of days, I think. I haven't gotten all the details yet." She glanced around the office to check that no one was listening. "It's BLC!" she whispered.

"Oh," I said. I didn't know what she meant.

"That's where I'm going," she explained. BLC must be a fairy godmother department. It sounded more like some kind of sandwich to me!

"Big Life Change," she explained.

"Oh, yes, of course," I said, feeling more and more obviously an absolute fraud with every passing moment.

"You haven't heard of it, then," she said. She looked disappointed.

"Well, I —"

"It's OK," she said. "I didn't expect you to have heard of it. Hardly anyone has. It's quite new. We help people who are adjusting to a new life."

"It sounds good," I said, meaning it.

"It'll be the first client assignment I've had for ages! I'm really looking forward to it."

Just then, my MagiCell beeped. "Looks like someone wants you," Tabitha said. "I'll leave you alone."

She disappeared back to her desk, and I looked at the screen. When I saw the words, my heart flipped over and doubled its pace. FG FOUND! it said in big bold letters. Underneath, another word: CONNECT?

I'd done it! I'd found Daisy! My heart beating so rapidly I felt as if it were going to fly out of my chest, I touched the screen. "Yes, connect!"

This was it. I was going to talk to Daisy and find out what had happened to Mom!

chapter six

Philippa

"Daisy?" I said uncertainly into the MagiCell. How did you speak into one of these, anyway? I held it like a walkie-talkie, talking into the speaker and then holding it up to my ear.

Nothing happened.

I checked to see that no one was watching me. I didn't want to look even more like a fool than I already did, with all the other things I'd gotten wrong.

I tried again. "This is Philippa calling Daisy," I said in a stage whisper. "Do you read me? Come in, Daisy."

Again, nothing. I was about to switch off the MagiCell and put it away when it suddenly crackled, then hissed, then hummed. And then — "Philippa?"

I gripped the MagiCell with both hands and whispered into it again. "Daisy! Is that really you?"

Daisy laughed. "I can't believe it's you," she said. "How did you —"

"It doesn't matter," I said. "I'll explain when I see you. What's happened with my mom?"

"We stopped it!" Daisy said. "The SRB — it's gone. Your mom's fine!"

I let out a breath that I felt I'd been holding since we'd gotten to ATC and tried to reply, but my answer got stuck in my throat.

"Philippa? Did you hear me?"

I swallowed hard and tried again. "Daisy, that's wonderful!" I said. "That's so great. Thank you *so* much!"

"How about you?" she asked. "Are you OK?"

"I'm fine. I can't believe I'm getting away with it, but so far so good. How are you doing there?"

"I love it!" she said. "Well, I mean, it's fine. It's OK."

"What are you doing now?"

"I'm in your room with Robyn."

A stab of jealousy went through me. Daisy and Robyn hanging out together in my room. Daisy there in the cottage with my mom and dad. Me stuck up here, with no idea what I was doing or how I was ever going to get out of this and return to my normal life. Suddenly, being able to fly around and talk to computers didn't feel quite so exciting anymore.

"Have you had any ideas about how to get me home yet?" I asked quietly.

There was a long pause at the other end. "I'm still trying to figure something out," she said eventually. "Listen, get in touch with me again in —"

Just then, a noise behind me snatched my attention away from what Daisy was saying. I looked around. It was Daisy's supervisor — and she was heading toward me!

"Daisy, I can't talk anymore," I whispered into the MagiCell.

"Why? What's up? Listen, all we need to do is —"

"Who are you talking to?" The supervisor's voice boomed across my head.

I looked up. "I — it's — I . . ." I said helpfully.

"Is that FG32561?" she asked. With a shudder of recognition, I realized what she was asking me.

FG32561 — that was the number I'd put into my MagiCell. She knew that I was talking to Daisy!

"Um, I —" I began. But it was too late. Before I could even think of anything to say, she had snatched the MagiCell from me and was talking into it. "I knew we would catch you this time," she snapped into the MagiCell. "FG32561, you have broken numerous FGC rules and you will not escape lightly. Do you hear me?"

The supervisor frowned as she held the MagiCell to her ear.

"Enough of your excuses," she snapped a moment later. "You are being stripped of your FG powers, with immediate effect. I'm going to speak to my superiors about this. I'll be sending someone to fetch you. Do you understand?"

Another pause. Another agonizing silence at my end.

"Good. I want you in my office first thing in the morning. First thing, you hear me?" And with that, she switched off the MagiCell and turned to me.

I shut my eyes. I don't know why. I mean, when you're really little, you think that if you close your eyes and can't see anyone, then they can't see you, either. I'm old enough to know it doesn't work like that — although I couldn't help wishing that perhaps it might. I was going to be in the biggest trouble I could imagine. In fact, probably *bigger* trouble than I could imagine. I wanted to cry. I wanted to go home. I wanted —

"You did very well, my newest young fairy," a voice was saying. It sounded like the supervisor, and it sounded like she was talking to me.

I half opened one of my eyes. She was still there. Right in front of me. And — wait a minute, what was she doing with her face? I hadn't seen her do that yet. She was smiling! At me!

What was going on? I opened both eyes and stared at her, still too shocked to speak.

"Modest as well," she said, nodding approvingly. "I will be sure to inform ATC High Command of that, too." She turned to leave, and I finally found my tongue.

"Wait!" I said. The supervisor slowly turned around. "I mean, please. If you don't mind. Thank you," I burbled.

She smiled another tight little smile at me. "Yes, dear?" she said.

"I — um, I'm not sure what it is exactly that you'll be telling High Command," I said, desperately trying to stop my nerves from making my voice come out sounding like a rattlesnake.

"Why, that you found our errant fairy," she said, "and now we may punish her accordingly."

Punish her accordingly? What had I done?

"But you — but, I mean, will you —"

The supervisor laughed. "Don't you worry, my dear," she said. "I know what you're trying to ask."

"You do?" I gulped. She knew I wanted to ask what kind of punishment Daisy was going to get? She knew I was terrified for the pair of us? She knew that I was desperately trying to stop myself from wondering how exactly they punished humans who broke into ATC?

"Of course." She smiled. "You're wondering what kind of reward you'll get."

"Am I?" I gasped. "I mean — yes. Yes, I am. Ha, ha, how did you guess?"

"And you'll be pleased to know that I will be highly commending you for your work," the supervisor went on. "You shall indeed be rewarded — have no worries. Now back to work, dear. I'm off to talk to ATC High Command."

And with that, she turned and left. And I sat at my desk, staring into space and wondering how I was ever going to get out of this mess.

Daisy

"Philippa? Philippa!" I shouted at my MagiCell, pressing every button, banging my hand against it, shaking it. Nothing.

"What is it?" Robyn asked. "What's happened?"

"Look." I showed her the MagiCell.

Robyn shook her head. "I don't understand."

"Look—the screen."

"I can't see anything. Just a blank space."

"Exactly." I flumped down on the bed. "It's shut off. I can't get reception or anything."

"Did the battery run out?" Robyn asked.

I shook my head. "MagiCells don't have batteries. It's my supervisor—she must have disabled it."

"Why?" Robyn asked, looking more closely at the Magi-Cell, turning it over in her hands.

"They've taken my FG powers away," I said. "They just want me safely back at ATC, sitting in front of them—awaiting my punishment." I shuddered.

"Your punishment?" Robyn asked. "What will they do?"

"You don't want to know," I said. "But put it this way—ATC High Command is not known for leniency."

"Oh, Daisy," she said. "I'm so sorry."

"What are *you* sorry for?"

Robyn shrugged. "I don't know. I just wish there was something I could do."

I smiled at her. "I know. It's OK." I got up and brushed myself off. "I'll be fine, honestly. You go. I don't want you worrying. I've already got Philippa caught up in all this." I shuddered again as I thought of her up there with FGRaincloud74921. What would they do to *her*? Had they discovered she was a human yet?

"You don't want me worrying?" Robyn said, shaking her head. "Daisy, we're in this together, the three of us, OK?"

I met her eyes and saw in them only concern—and friendship. "OK," I agreed. "Thank you."

"You don't need to thank me," Robyn replied. "You just need to help me figure this out."

"Figure what out?"

"Think about it," she said. "Once you've left, that's it. No Philippa, no you. How am I supposed to explain that Philippa's disappeared again?"

She was right. Once I was gone, there were no guarantees I'd *ever* be able to get back! And we still had no idea how to get Philippa back, either. Her situation was probably even more bleak than it had been before. Now that she'd been caught in contact with me, who knew what ATC would do?

"What do we do, then?" I asked helplessly.

Robyn thought for a moment, her eyes scrunched up as she concentrated. "I've got an idea," she said a few moments later. "Listen, we need to buy some time, right?"

"Right," I agreed.

"OK, so tomorrow is New Year's Eve. There's always a big party up near Tidehill Rocks with fireworks and a bonfire and stuff. The whole village comes. It's amazing."

"OK," I said uncertainly. I couldn't exactly see how a great big party fit in with a plan to get us out of trouble with ATC!

"So, try to get some sleep tonight, then I'll come to get you in the morning. We'll tell Philippa's mom and dad that we're preparing for the party all day tomorrow," Robyn went on. "My dad's one of the organizers this year, so we can say we're helping him. Then we just tell Philippa's parents you'll come to the party with us and meet them there. That gives us twenty-four hours from now." She smiled nervously. "Do you think that'll be enough time?"

Twenty-four *hours*? I didn't know how to respond. Laugh hysterically at the mere suggestion of fixing this mess in the space of a day? Throw myself on the floor and cry like a baby? Give up completely? In the end, I looked at her face, and when I saw the hope in her eyes, I knew there was only one response I could give.

"I think that's a great idea," I said.

Robyn responded with a bright, confident smile, and we went downstairs to ask Mr. and Mrs. Fisher if I could spend tomorrow helping out with Robyn. After today's events, they took some persuading. We had to promise not to go anywhere near that path and to stay near Robyn's dad all day. In the end, they agreed.

And when it was bedtime and they both gave me enormous hugs and put Philippa's new pajamas out for me and told me how much they loved me, I got that warm feeling again—and I couldn't help thinking that perhaps everything just might turn out OK.

ATC
HIGH COMMAND

The ALD supervisor, FGRaincloud74921, bowed low in front of her superiors. "FG32561 is due in my office first thing in the morning. If I might be permitted to offer an opinion, given this fairy's previous misdemeanors, I would suggest that she be given the harshest of punishments. And this is my newest recruit, who helped us find the errant fairy," she said, holding out her MagiCell to show her superiors a picture of the heroic young fairy.

The two night stars looked at the picture on the screen, and then at each other. To an observer, the slight nod which passed between them would most certainly have passed for an agreement with FGRaincloud's proposal for punishing FG32561.

To them, however, the nod meant something quite different.

"We are delighted with your work," FGNightstar90034 said with a smile so bright, the room twinkled and sparkled. "But we would like to deal with this fairy ourselves. We will have her brought directly to us in the morning."

"Would you like me to see her first, so I can give her an indication of the severity of her punishment?" FGRaincloud74921 asked with a lick of her lips, as though thirsty for blood.

FGNightstar27785 shook her head. "That won't be necessary," she said. "We'll take it from here."

The interview was clearly over, and with a brief nod, an awkward curtsy, and a swift exit, FGRaincloud74921 returned to her post in ALD.

The two senior High Command officials sat in silence for a moment as they waited for the door to close behind the supervisor.

The conversation they were about to have needed absolute privacy.

"It's a miracle!"

"I'll say. At the eleventh hour, as well!"

"This could be just what we've been looking for."

"Let's hope so. It's our last option."

"I know. It's getting hard to put up a normal front. If word gets out about our situation, we'll have no way of stopping the panic."

"But can you imagine FGRaincloud74921 not spotting the truth about her new fairy godmother?"

"To be fair, without seeing the picture, we wouldn't have known ourselves—and even then it's only because we've recently come across her in our research."

"True. And now the pair of them have been virtually delivered to our door. Let's get on with it."

"Wait. The stakes are so high, and we need to be sure they're up to this. We can't afford a failure."

"How about putting them both to the test first, to make sure they are the ones?"

"Good idea. If they don't pass the highest loyalty test, we don't go through with it."

"Let's hope they pass, then. For all of our sakes. If they don't . . ."

"No—don't say it. We can't even contemplate failure. If this fails, we're all in more trouble than we could even imagine."

"You're right. Let's do it. First thing in the morning, we get that fairy in here and get this thing going, before it's too late—for all of us."

Daisy

It was eight in the morning and still dark when Robyn called for me. I left a note for Philippa's parents, since they were both snoring and dead to the world.

Closing the front door softly behind me, I followed Robyn down the driveway and we headed to the woods.

"This is it," I said when we got to the stone circle. "You'd better go now, before they get here."

"Who's *they*?" she asked.

I frowned. "I don't know. They'll send someone to collect me."

"Because they took your transportation powers away, along with everything else?"

"Exactly."

"I hope they send someone nice," Robyn said.

"Yeah, me too." *Not likely*, I added silently.

Robyn pulled her coat close around her. "Will I have any way of knowing what's going on?" she asked.

"I don't know," I said. "I don't think so. I'm really sorry."

"OK," Robyn said, doing about as good a job as I was at hiding her feelings. I hated leaving her like this, without knowing what would happen or when she might see me—or Philippa—again. Then she turned to leave. "Hey, maybe I could talk to Annie?" she asked.

"Annie? What for?" Annie had already helped us once when Robyn's dad had trapped me in a jar.

"I don't know. Just—well, remember when you left us last time, Annie told you she would always make sure you were all right? Maybe she'll help us now. I could ask her."

I let out a breath. "I don't know," I said. "I'm not sure we should be involving her. I wouldn't want to get her in trouble with ATC, too."

"OK, I understand. I won't do anything now," she said. "But if things get really bad, if for any reason we really need her . . ."

"Yeah," I replied, not wanting her to finish her sentence any more than she did. "If worse comes to worst, I'm sure Annie will be there for us. If you get desperate, you could see if she knows anything."

Robyn nodded. "Good luck," she said, turning back around to wave.

I waved back, feeling wooden and cold. "You too," I said, forcing my mouth into a smile. "Go on. I'll be fine."

Robyn nodded and then, pulling her coat around her once more, she turned and walked away.

chapter seven

Philippa

"Wow, look at you!" Tabitha had poked her head over the divide and was grinning at me.

I guessed she was referring to the fact that I looked like someone who'd been up half the night. I should have slept like a baby. I was given a room of my own at ALD with every comfort I could imagine. That was the problem — like everything else up here, you just had to imagine it, and it was there. But I couldn't imagine anything! All my mind could focus on was the questions and worries swirling around in my head. What were they going to do with Daisy? How long would it be till I was found out? And when I was, what would they do with *me*?

I tried to look calm, and tried to smile at Tabitha, but I'm sure I failed miserably on both counts. "Look at me? Why?" I asked.

"You haven't even been here a whole day, and you're up for promotion already!" Tabitha said.

"Promotion?"

"That's what I just heard." Tabitha came over to my desk and went on. "I overheard Supervisor Raincloud74921 talking to someone about it. She was trying to claim the credit for herself. Said she'd handpicked you to join the department—which is quite funny considering she hadn't even realized you were joining us!"

"Oh, yes, ha, ha, that is funny, Tabitha," I said, trying to sound vaguely jovial.

"Tabby. That's what my friends call me," she said with a slight blush. "If we're friends, that is."

I smiled genuinely for the first time since Daisy had left. "Of course we are," I said. "So tell me, Tabby, what else have you heard?"

"Well, I heard something about you finding a fairy who's broken a whole bunch of FGC rules."

"Mm-hmm," I said, biting my tongue to stop myself from shouting, *"That's my friend you're talking about, and she did it for a good reason, you know!"*

Tabby obviously hadn't even realized that the fairy who was on her way back to ATC to be punished was the same one who'd brought me up here only yesterday.

Tabby leaned in closer. "And I heard something else," she whispered, her eyes shining with the excitement of her news. With a quick look around to check that no one was listening, she went on. "I heard that there's a *human* up here!"

"A — a —" I couldn't find any more words. What was I supposed to say to *that*?

"I know. Isn't it the most outrageous thing you've ever heard? Imagine a human getting into ATC! No one knows how it happened, or even where the human is — but some of the systems have registered its presence."

"*Its?*" I asked before I could stop myself.

"The human's! They'll find it soon enough and dispose of it somehow — but what a scandal, right?"

"Yeah!" I said. "Ha! What a scandal!" I couldn't really say anything else for a while. All I could think about was the phrase *"dispose of it somehow."*

What would she think if she knew it was me she was talking about?

Tabby shook her head and went on. "You know, it's hard to even imagine it now, isn't it? I mean, fairies and humans having the kind of friendships we used to have back in the old days."

I didn't get it. It was their job to try and make sure things went smoothly for us. Why did they do it when so many of them didn't seem to like us? I wanted to ask her — but I knew I couldn't.

"Um . . . yeah," I said, wishing I had a clue what she was talking about.

She looked indignant. "But it's not our fault it changed, is it? After all, it's the humans who let *us* down, who forgot about *us*, stopped believing in *us*, forgot about the symbols of friendship that we'd built *together*. It's not the fairies who moved on and left them behind. And yet we're still the ones who keep doing everything we can for them. We've never gone back on our side of the bargain, and we never will. Honestly, it's not surprising if every now and then we get a bit touchy about it!"

I paused to take in what she'd said. Her answer had half answered the question I'd wanted to ask — but in the process it had opened up about fifty more! What bargain? If only I could ask her more about it — but how could I, without making her suspicious?

"Yes, I suppose I see what you're saying," I said eventually. "And of course, I feel that way too, quite often." I really couldn't think of anything more convincing to say. But I was intrigued. Fairies and humans had once been friends? If it had been that way in the past, maybe sometime in the future it could be like that again. Perhaps one day, fairies wouldn't get into enormous trouble just for trying to help a human out.

The last thought brought me back down to my current reality.

As if on cue, the supervisor appeared at the end of the corridor — and she was heading our way.

"Now then, my little gem," she said, straightening her already impeccable suit and flicking a nonexistent bit of fluff from her shoulder. I looked around to see who she was calling a gem. A second later, she was at my desk. "You're to come with me," she said — to me! "You're wanted at High Command."

I got up from my desk and followed her, trying to ignore the looks I got from the other fairies all the way down the aisle, and trying to stop my legs from giving way beneath me. We reached the wall, and the supervisor nodded briefly at it. The wall shimmered and wobbled in front of me. "Good luck," she said. And with that, she nudged me toward the wall.

Closing my eyes, I took a couple of steps, hoping I wasn't about to walk into a wall in front of the whole office. But I didn't. The wall dissolved around me, zipping shut the second I'd walked through it. I turned around. FGRaincloud74921 was gone. The office was gone. I was in a white, bare corridor. At the end of it, a door stood open. I walked toward it. Inside, two stars twinkled and shone so brightly, I had to shield my eyes.

Then one of them spoke!

"Don't be shy," it said. "Come in. Come a bit closer."

I walked toward the star. The door closed behind me as a chair appeared out of nowhere.

"Sit," the other one said.

I sat down in the chair.

"Now then," said the first star, and while I was trying furiously to stop myself from contemplating how they were going to "dispose" of me, the star added, "We've got a job for you."

"So, let me just make sure I've got this right," I said. The stars had explained what my job was — and I didn't have a clue how to respond. "Because of my good work for ALD in catching an errant fairy, I am going to be rewarded and promoted?"

"Correct," said the first star with a slight twinkle.

"But before that, you want me to go down to Earth, collect the fairy, and bring her back to you so she can be punished accordingly."

The second star twinkled even more strongly. "Also correct."

I paused before saying anything else. They wanted me to personally go down to Earth and collect Daisy so she could face the worst punishment of her life. And if I didn't want to? I had the feeling this wasn't a polite request — and I knew from Daisy that you don't turn down orders from ATC High Command.

"OK, then," I said. The only other problem was the small matter of my not having any idea how to get down to Earth. If I knew that, we wouldn't have been in this mess in the first place.

"We will transport you to the portal," one of the stars went on as if it had read my thoughts. "From there, we want you to take this for FG32561 to get back here."

At that moment, something appeared out of nowhere and floated over toward me. It landed on my knee.

"A box?" I asked.

"Open it."

I lifted the lid, and a waft of multicolored smoke billowed out like a silk scarf on a breeze. As the colors floated around the box, a piece of parchment floated out and mingled in among the colors. I looked up at the stars.

"Read it."

I snatched the piece of parchment and read aloud.

> Go to the highest ring of stones,
> And read aloud this rhyme.
> Call out the numbers that you see,
> And travel just one time.

I looked inside the box. There was nothing else. No numbers.

"Where are the —" I began.

"The numbers will appear when you are at the portal. Recite the poem, and they will flow out with the colors. When FG32561 says them out loud, she can cross over. She is to use this to come back to ATC. We will take it from there."

"Right," I said, placing the parchment back inside

the box. The colors instantly floated back inside, and I closed the lid. "Right," I said again, not really knowing what else to say.

The stars said nothing more. Their light was fading. The interview was over.

I backed toward the door. "OK, well, thank you," I said, opening the door and letting myself out.

As soon as I was through the door, it disappeared and I was alone in the vast white emptiness of ATC High Command. My knees gave way as I thought about what I had to do. I could hardly think of a worse punishment. Find my best friend — and bring her in to be punished.

I didn't have long to think about it. Within moments of my leaving the room, two figures approached me — out of nowhere, like everything else around here. As they came toward me, I saw that they were young men, boys, not much older than me. It hadn't occurred to me that fairy godmothers could be male. I guess they'd be fairy godfathers or godbrothers or something.

Smiling, they approached me and both shook my hand. "Well done," one of them said as we walked along the corridor together. "Very impressive work you did there. We do like to see them caught like that, especially when they think they're being so clever."

"Mm," I said.

"Makes our day, that does," the other one said. "It's generally a bit dull at RPD. Not usually all that much happening."

"RPD?" I said, hoping it wasn't something *else* that I should have known.

"Retrieval and Punishment Department," the first one said lightly.

"Typical," the other one said with a wink. "No one's ever heard of us!" Then he led us around a corner to a new corridor. "Shortcut," he explained, and I followed in silence.

As we walked, I realized I'd been here already. It was the same corridor Daisy and I had come through when we'd arrived at ATC. Or a similar one, anyway. Bright white, spotless, and completely empty, except for us. It seemed to go on forever.

After we'd been walking for a while, the boys came to an abrupt halt. "Well, this is our stop," one of them said. "Do you want us to wait here for you, in case she gives you any trouble?"

"No, I'll be fine," I said, trying to smile reassuringly at them. The last thing I wanted was to be escorted straight back to those stars with Daisy. I'm not sure what they had in mind if Daisy caused "trouble," but I didn't want to find out.

"You've got the code?" the other boy asked.

I patted the box under my arm.

"We'll leave you to it, then," he said. "Good luck."

"Thank you," I said with what I hoped was an efficient nod. I waved awkwardly at them. "See you later."

They waved back. Then in unison, they turned around, walked a few paces — and disappeared.

I let out a breath. I was on my own.

I turned slowly around. All I could see was blank white space. Which way was I meant to go? Where was the door to the portal?

Then I remembered how all the other doors worked around here. Without stopping to question myself, in case the smallest amount of doubt squashed the idea, I stepped confidently forward and walked into the wall.

Instantly it dissolved, flowing into a bubbly, spongy mist. Which was quite a relief, I have to say, as I didn't need to add a few broken limbs to my problems.

I walked through the mist and out the other side—and emerged into pitch darkness.

There was no floor, no wall, no ceiling—nothing. I was standing on pure black space! A complete void surrounded me. I gave myself up to the fact that I had no idea where I was, how I'd gotten here, and how—or even *if*—I would ever get out of it.

Then I heard a voice.

"Philippa?"

Daisy! I peered into the darkness. Still I couldn't see a thing. Could she see me? Was she in here with me? "Daisy?" I called back uncertainly.

"I'm on the other side," she said.

"Other side of what?"

"The tunnel."

"Tunnel? What tunnel?"

"At the portal. The stone circle."

"I don't remember a tunnel at the stone circle," I called.

"It's not a normal tunnel—the kind you dig underground."

"What other kinds of tunnels are there?" I asked.

"Fairy ones," Daisy replied. "You came through this one when we went to ATC together, except you didn't realize it because you had me there to lead you through."

"Through? Through what?"

"Close your eyes," Daisy called.

I did as she said.

"Keep them closed until you can picture a tunnel," she said. "Visualize it: You're at one end of it, and it's long and dark, but you can see the light at the other end. You can see a hole ahead of you. When you can see that hole, open your eyes."

I concentrated on picturing a tunnel. Once I was sure I could see a light at the other end, I opened my eyes.

The darkness had lifted! I could see the hole at the end of the tunnel—and Daisy was in the middle of it, waving and grinning at me!

"Daisy!" I ran toward her. But nothing was happening. I could feel my feet and legs moving; I could even *see* them moving. But I wasn't getting anywhere. "I can't reach you," I said. "Why isn't it working?"

Daisy's smile dropped. "I don't know," she said. "Well, I probably do. I don't think you can come out this way."

"Why?"

"It's because you're a human."

"But I've done all sorts of things at ATC!" I said. "I've even flown! I know how to do the thinking thing."

Daisy shook her head. "I guess humans don't have the power to go through the fairy portals by themselves."

"So I can't get to you?" I said, trying not to think about what else this meant. That I couldn't get back to Earth, back home, back to my parents. Could I even get back to ATC or would I be stuck here forever, spinning slowly around in the huge vast emptiness of space?

"You can only go back through the tunnel, but not out this way, I guess," Daisy said. "And I can't get to you, either, since they've taken my fairy godmother powers away. In fact" — Daisy paused — "how did you even get here?"

Which was when I remembered what I was here for. I held the box out in front of me. "Daisy, I've got something for you," I said nervously.

Daisy smiled. "You brought me a present?"

"Not exactly." I grimaced. "They told me to bring it here."

"Who's they?" Daisy asked, the smile disappearing as she saw the look on my face.

"Um, RPD."

"RPD — Retrieval and Punishment Department? What have they done to you? Philippa, are you OK? Are you being punished for helping me?" Daisy's questions came out in such a rush, I didn't know which one to answer first.

"Daisy," I said eventually. "They don't want to punish me at all."

Daisy smiled brightly. "Well that's great! That's — oh." Her face fell as she realized what I was saying. "You're here for me, aren't you?" she said. "You've come to collect me."

"It's High Command. They want you. They don't even realize I'm human," I said. "They think I found you on purpose. They're going to *reward* me!" I hated saying all this to Daisy, but she was my best friend. I wasn't going to hide it from her.

"It's OK, I understand," Daisy said quietly. "And it's still great that they haven't found out about you yet." She nodded at the box. "So what's in there?"

I looked at the box. "It's got a poem inside it. It's for you," I said.

"A PTC," Daisy said. "Portal Transfer Code," she explained when she saw the blank look on my face. "It's for getting across a portal when there's no other method available. You use it once and then it vanishes. They want you to give it to me so I can get back."

"So they can punish you," I said.

"I guess so." Daisy looked about as glum as I felt.

"Look, here's what we should do," I said, determined to do *something* to help. "You come back, and we go to ATC together. I'm not going to abandon you. I'm not letting you face them without me. I'll tell them why you did what you did, how you were trying to help, how the whole thing is practically my fault, and —"

"Philippa, the whole thing *isn't* practically your fault!" Daisy interrupted me. "It wasn't *you* who chose to break one of the most important rules of FGC. You didn't force me to come down to Earth, to disguise myself so I could make contact with you. You didn't even know I was doing that! No, I'm not letting you take the blame. Anyway, I've got a better idea."

"What's that?" I asked.

Daisy paused for a moment before saying, "You use it."

"Use what?"

"The code. It's a one-way trip, one use only, and will work for whoever says the code. This could be your one and only chance to get back to Earth! Philippa, you have no choice. You have to use it. Come back here and get on with your life."

"What? Get on with my life? How could I do that, knowing that you've just put yourself in even *more* trouble to help me again?"

"You have to use it," Daisy insisted. "If you don't, it'll only be a matter of time before they find you out — and it's not even worth thinking about what they'll do to you when they discover that you broke into ATC."

"I didn't break in! I just read the poem on the rock!"

"It doesn't matter. That's not how they'll see it. I know how it works. ATC is a good place, and we do brilliant things — but the rules are strict, and the people who enforce them are even stricter."

I thought about what she was saying. This might be my only chance to get back down to

Earth. I could use the code and be home in minutes! The thought was *so* appealing. Except for one thing.

Daisy would be stuck on Earth, too — and it wouldn't be long before ATC sent someone else after her. Someone who would do the job properly and bring her back to face her punishment — and the punishment would be even *worse* once they found out she'd avoided being brought back to them once. No, I wasn't going to do it. Daisy had risked more than enough already. I wasn't going to let her put herself on the line for me again.

"I'm not going to use the code," I said firmly. "I'm not deserting you. We'll go to ATC together. I don't care what it takes or what happens to me, I'm not abandoning you. OK?"

Daisy looked at me for a moment. Then she smiled and lowered her head. "OK," she said softly. "Thank you."

I held the box out. "Are you ready?" I asked.

Daisy opened her mouth to reply — but suddenly stopped. "No! Wait!" she said. "Look, I've got another idea. A compromise."

"Daisy, there's no compromise. You've already said how strict ATC is."

"I think I can get back another way," she said. "Hold on to the code. We'll face ATC together like you said. But once we know what they're going to do with me, and once we know we can do it without causing any more trouble, you use the code to come back to Earth. OK?"

"How will you get back, though?" I asked.

"Annie," Daisy said simply. "It was Robyn who reminded me — Annie said she'll always be there for me. We know we can trust her. She can help me get back, I'm sure of it."

Daisy was already moving away from the light. "Look, stay there. Wait for me. I'll run to Annie's and see if she can do this. If not, I'll use the portal code, but please, let me try this first. Just wait for me, OK?"

I nodded. "OK," I said. "But hurry."

A moment later, Daisy was gone, and I was left alone, silently waiting in the vast black emptiness of the portal's void.

Daisy

It took longer than I'd expected to get Annie to help. Not that she was being unhelpful — she just wanted to understand the ins and outs of the whole thing so she knew what she was getting involved with.

We sat at her kitchen table, and I told her everything. As much of it as I could, anyway. I still didn't know what had been going on with Philippa up at ATC. All I knew was that I had to get back there before they realized what she was doing.

Finally, I'd told Annie the whole story. She breathed out and shook her head. "I hope you know what you've gotten yourself into," she said gently. From anyone else, it might have sounded like a warning. From Annie, I knew it was just her way of showing she cared.

"I do," I said. "But right now, all that matters is that I need to get back before Philippa's found out."

Annie got up and climbed her stepladder to reach a jar on the top shelf. "Good thing I held on to this. Just promise me you won't do anything silly," she said. "Anything sillier than what you've already done."

I shook my head. "I won't."

Annie poured the contents of the jar into a small bottle. A smell of jasmine and roses wafted around the kitchen as mauve and pink bubbles frothed around the top of the jar. "Drink this when you get to the portal," she said, putting a lid on the bottle and closing it tight. "It will get you across."

I took the bottle from her. "Thank you," I said, getting up.

"Annie, I wasn't here, OK?"

"What do you mean?"

"You've already done so much for me—I don't want to risk getting you in trouble with ATC, too."

Before she could respond, I ran out the door, clutching a bottle of magic vapors in my hand and praying I got to Philippa before anyone else did.

chapter eight

Philippa

Something was happening on the other side. Movement of some sort. Daisy — she was back! But what was she doing? She had a bottle in her hands and was taking the lid off. Bright colors spilled out of the bottle as soon as she'd opened it. Then she tipped the bottle up to her mouth and drank the contents.

Moments later, I watched her step forward — and enter the tunnel.

"You made it!" I said, letting out a breath that I felt I'd been holding for the last hour.

"I told you I would." She moved away and indicated for me to come with her. "Come on, follow me," she said. "Just keep walking in the darkness, and I'll lead us back out."

"Out?" I said hopefully. Had she found a way for us to escape from this mess?

Daisy glanced at me. "I mean back to ATC."

"Oh, yes. Of course."

I followed Daisy step by step into the void until, finally, the darkness began to lift. Before I knew it, we were back in the white corridor.

Daisy stopped. "Philippa, listen. Please. You shouldn't come with me. There's no need for you to get into trouble."

"I'm coming," I said firmly. "I told you, you're not doing this on your own. I'm going to be beside you every step of the —"

"There she is!"

I spun around to see the two fairy godbrothers from RPD heading toward us. My first instinct was to run. My second instinct was to wave in what I hoped was a casual manner. On reflection, I imagine I probably looked more like someone flailing her arms in the air while drowning, but let's face it — the thought of what lay ahead wasn't exactly relaxing.

"Oh, hi there," I said with the same attempting-casual-but-probably-failing-badly manner. "Just on our way up to High Command. See you there."

The two fairy godbrothers looked at me. Then they looked at each other. Then they marched straight over to Daisy. One on either side of her, they took hold of her arms and started flying away with her.

"Hey!" I called to their retreating backs. "Where are you going?"

"High Command," one of them called without turning around.

"Hold on, I'm coming too!" I called, trying to catch up. But no matter how fast I tried to go, they were professional fliers and I was still learning. They were still ahead of me and rapidly getting farther and farther away.

"It's fine; you're not needed anymore," one of them shouted over his shoulder to me. Nice.

"You're welcome, by the way!" I called — but they were virtually out of sight.

Now what? I stood watching them for a moment — and then I made up my mind. I'd promised Daisy I'd be there for her when she faced her punishment, and

I *wasn't* going to let her down. I knew where they were heading — the room with the stars inside it. I just had to find it again — on foot. Well, that's what I would do. I *had* to help. I *had* to get Daisy out of this!

Daisy

I waited in the holding area outside High Command, my head spinning with questions. What were they going to do to me? What would happen to Philippa? Would she be found out?

A light shone under the doorframe. Then the door opened and the light reached around and beckoned me in. This was it. Time to find out exactly what happened when you broke pretty much every rule in the Fairy Godmother Code.

I went inside and closed the door behind me.

"Do you know why you are here?" The star's voice was cold and brittle, like a shard of ice.

I nodded. I kept my head down. I couldn't bear to face that glare, the disappointment and anger behind it.

The next voice was softer. "We're on your side," the second star said. So that was how they did things around here:

bad star/good star, like you get good cop/bad cop teams in those police dramas. Reel you in, make you feel comfortable, then *wham*! Hit you with your punishment.

It was so ridiculous, I nearly laughed. The only thing that stopped me was the absolute certainty that if I did, it would come out as a hysterical cry that I'd have no way of stopping.

Then the first star spoke again. But the weird thing was, her voice was just as soft. *Good star and good star?* "We mean it," she said gently.

I opened my eyes. They had both materialized as people! I couldn't believe it! There they were in front of me, both sitting back in big cozy armchairs. Two kindly, middle-aged women with laugh lines and smiling eyes. What was going on?

I tried to sit up straighter and found that my chair had transformed into one the same as theirs. I couldn't help relaxing into the comfy warmth of it.

The women both smiled at me. "We have a suggestion for you," one of them said. She held her smile, but something told me she was faking it. I'd broken *huge* rules. I was due for one of the biggest punishments they could think of. Unless this was what they were like before they terminated you altogether.

"You have a choice," the fairy went on. "You *can* face a Level One punishment if you choose."

Level One? That was the worst! "Or?" I asked nervously.

The second fairy leaned forward in her chair. As far as she could on something bouncy and fluffy, anyway. "Or you could do something for us. One small favor and this whole thing is forgotten."

"Forgotten?" I asked. "As in, disappears?"

She nodded. "As in, we wipe the slate clean and say no more about any of your misdemeanors."

"Ever?"

"Ever."

"I'll do it!" I said. I didn't care what the favor was. Nothing could be worse than a Level One punishment! One small favor, she said, and I was off the hook. It was a no-brainer. A no-winger, a no-*anything*er! I wanted to jump up and fly around the room; I wanted to run down the corridor shouting; I wanted to find Philippa and tell her; I wanted to—

"There is a human at ATC," the first fairy said. Her smile had dropped but her eyes still looked kind.

"We want you to find her," the second one continued.

"Mm-hmm," I said. I didn't trust myself to use actual words.

"You know how we feel about having humans at ATC," the fairy went on. "It is not acceptable."

"Absolutely not," I said as convincingly as I could.

"And you know how we must punish them once we've found them," the first one said.

I cleared my throat to hide a small yelp. "Um, remind me?"

The fairy laughed. "Oh, no. The punishment for a human at ATC is not something you say out loud."

"Let's just call it *unspeakable*," the other one added.

"Unspeakable." I gulped.

"You have one hour," the first fairy said. "Bring us the human." And with that, they both turned back into stars, transformed my chair into a stool so hard that I fell right off it, and shone their starlight at me so brightly, I had to shield my eyes.

Interview over, I guessed. My task had begun. I had one hour—to find my best friend and bring her in for an "unspeakable" punishment.

I left High Command in a complete daze. My brain wouldn't do anything except run the same thought around and around again, over and over. After all this, my one way out of facing the worst punishment imaginable was to subject my best friend to it instead.

Philippa was there waiting for me at ALD.

"I tried to follow you but they wouldn't let me in," she said. "The guards brought me back here. I've been so worried. How are you? What happened?"

I tried to laugh off her barrage of questions. "Hey, I'm fine," I said, looking everywhere except at her. "Couldn't be better." I tried a quick smile, but it probably looked more like the kind of expression they'd use on a poster for a horror movie.

"Anyway, I'd better get to work," I said briskly. "Lots to catch up on. Talk to you later."

And then I flipped a few folders over and shuffled some papers around and stared hard at the blank screen on my computer.

"Daisy, what is it?" Philippa asked gently. "What happened? Why are you being weird?"

"I'm not being weird," I said. Why wouldn't she go away? I needed to think. "Not weird at all. Just working. Lots to do." I stared harder at my computer, frowning at it as though it contained the most important and interesting piece of information I'd ever seen. I hit a few keys on my keyboard, so she could see how hard I was working.

"Daisy," Philippa said.

I tried to ignore her.

"Daisy!" she said more firmly.

I tore my eyes away from the screen and turned to face her. "What? You'll have to be quick, because I really have lots of work."

Philippa nudged a finger toward my computer screen. "It's not even on," she said.

I looked again at the screen. Then I looked at Philippa. Then I looked down at my desk.

"Daisy, what is it? What's your punishment? I'm really sorry." Philippa's voice was so gentle I thought it was going to break me in two. "It's all my fault," she went on. "I'd do anything to help. I'd face the punishment *myself* if I could!"

She looked at me with such big, honest eyes, and with the kind of friendship I've never had with anyone else, and in that moment I realized what I had to do.

I smiled at Philippa. "Thank you!" I said, jumping out of my chair.

"What for?" Philippa asked. "I'm only saying the truth. That's what friendship's about, isn't it?"

"Yes. Yes it is!" I said, for the first time in days feeling happy and excited. "I'd almost forgotten!"

I tidied my desk and headed down the corridor. "I'll see you in a bit," I said, desperately hoping I would. Who knew what I was going to face for doing this?

"Where are you going?" Philippa called as I hurried out of ALD.

"Just got to talk to someone," I called back. Well, to two people. Two stars, to be precise.

I was going to tell them they could get someone else to do their dirty work. They could punish me as much as they wanted. I wasn't going to betray Philippa. Nothing they could do to me would *ever* make me do that.

ATC

HIGH COMMAND

"So that's it—that's all there is to it," FG32561 said defiantly. "You can do whatever you want with me, but I am declining your assignment, thank you."

She stood in front of the two High Command officials, her knees shaking so much it was a wonder her legs were managing to hold her up straight. But still, she spoke with conviction.

The two stars—two of the highest ranking officials in the whole of ATC—turned to each other and nodded.

At this tiny gesture, the young fairy closed her eyes and swallowed hard.

Then one of the fairies spoke.

"Wait outside," she said.

FG32561 did not need to be asked twice. She shot out of the room as quickly as her terrified body could manage.

Once the door was closed behind her, the stars turned to each other again. This time, their smiles were so bright, the room was ablaze with twinkling light. The older one spoke first. "We've found them," she said. "They are exactly what we need."

"And just in time!" the other replied. "Let's get them back in here, and get the *real* assignment started."

And with that, word was instantly issued to their staff. "Bring FG32561 back in the room. And that new fairy at ALD—the one that located FG32561—bring her to us as well. Immediately."

chapter nine

Philippa

I bit my nails, twirled my hair, hummed quietly to myself, and looked at my watch again.

Only a minute had passed since I'd last looked. Where *was* she? What was going on? Why hadn't she told me what she was going to do? I couldn't stand the thought of Daisy getting into any more trouble — and I couldn't bear not knowing what had happened to her.

I was on the verge of going off to look for her when the door at the end of the office materialized — and the two male fairies about my age walked in.

They looked slowly around the whole office. Then they spotted me and instantly headed my way.

I gulped hard and tried to focus. I'd said I'd rather take the punishment than have Daisy face it herself — maybe that was exactly what was going to happen. I'd obviously put the thought into Daisy's head, and she'd put it into action!

No! She wouldn't do that — would she?

The fairy godbrothers had arrived at my desk and indicated for me to follow them out of the office.

"We've been sent to get you," one of them said. And without another word, they escorted me from my desk, along the corridor, and out of the office.

"Good luck!" Tabby whispered as I passed her. I tried to smile at her, but as with everything else I'd attempted since I'd been here, I failed.

"We'll get straight to the point," the fairy said. She told us she was called Alya. I was only half listening at this point. The other half of me was trying to communicate with Daisy. She was here, too! We'd been summoned together. At least that told me one thing. Whatever was happening, we were in it together. She hadn't pushed me forward for punishment instead of herself. I knew she wouldn't have, really. I felt disloyal for even having let the thought cross my mind.

The other fairy spoke. She was called Chara. "But first, sit down," she said.

Er, on what? There weren't any chairs! But when I looked again, a pair of comfy chairs had appeared behind us. And then a table appeared in front of us, with two steaming cups of hot chocolate and a plate of cookies.

"Help yourselves," Chara added.

Was it a trick? We'd broken some of their most important rules, and they were offering us cocoa and cookies?

"We'll wait," Daisy said firmly. "Let's hear what you have to say to us first."

"I agree," I said — even though the hot chocolate did smell *really* nice.

"Very well," Alya said. "We've brought you here because of the way you have both acted."

"Philippa's done nothing wrong!" Daisy said.

"Neither has Daisy," I added quickly. "Everything she's done is because of how good and how loyal she is, nothing else."

Alya held up a hand. "Wait, wait," she said calmly.

"We know all this," Chara said. "You have both acted exactly how we wanted you to act."

"*Wanted* us to act?" I said. "What do you mean?"

The fairy looked at me. "You refused to use the code to get you back to Earth, so you could stand by your friend's side if she was in trouble."

"How do you —"

Chara ignored me. "And you" — she turned to Daisy — "refused to turn your friend in. We know about all of it."

"But how?" Daisy asked. "How do you know? And if you know about it, what are we doing sitting here being offered drinks and sweets?"

"We know," replied Alya, "because we set it up."

I have to say, I was quite glad I *hadn't* helped myself to the hot chocolate, because at that point I think I might have spurted it out all over the fairies.

"You set it up?" Daisy asked, her face a picture of baffled disbelief. "But why? *How?* If you knew that Philippa was the human, why did you send me off to find her? Why did you —"

The fairy interrupted her with another silencing hand. "Wait," she said. "We'll tell you everything."

Daisy glanced at me. I gave a quick nod. "OK," Daisy said, folding her arms. "We're listening."

"First — neither of you is in any trouble," Alya began in a soft voice. It felt soothing and warm — a bit like the hot chocolate, which we'd decided to drink after all. "Quite the contrary," she went on. "You are a very special pair. Unique, in fact."

She took a sip of her drink. "Let's go back a few thousand years. A long, long time ago, humans and fairies were very great friends. They had friendships like you would not imagine." Alya paused and smiled at us both. "Friendships that *most* could not imagine, anyway," she said. "You two can probably imagine their friendships perfectly. Our tests have proved this."

"Your tests?" Daisy burst out. "You've been playing games with us?"

"Believe me, this is anything but a game," Alya said seriously. "The tests we carried out were to ensure that we were right about you. That you had the kind of friendship that is needed."

"Needed for what?" I asked.

"For an assignment that could save all of us," Alya said gravely. "Listen. I'll explain."

I shut my mouth tight and listened to what she had to say.

"Many, many years ago, humans and fairies worked together on all sorts of things. Among these were the portals." She turned to me. "In your world, they are known today as stone circles, ancient monuments whose history is unknown. The old days are so long forgotten now that many theories abound about the stone circles — their origin, their purpose. It is only the fairies who remember their true use. Indeed, today it is only fairies who can use them at all." Alya glanced at me. "It is only fairies who can *intentionally* use them," she corrected herself. "If a human gets caught up in some of the ancient magic, there is nothing we can do to prevent it from working. But this very rarely happens. So rarely, in fact, that most of us at ATC had forgotten it was even possible."

"But not you?" I said.

Alya shook her head. "Even we at High Command paid very little attention to the portals anymore — until recently."

"The stone circles were built as portals to allow fairies and humans to travel between each other's worlds," Chara went on. "But they were also a testament to the friendships between these fairies and humans. Because of this, only those with the greatest bonds of friendship were able to take part in their construction, or their continued upkeep. The friendship sealed the stones in place more solidly than any cement or mortar. The friendship was what really made the circles magical. So, the human and fairy relationships and the magic contained in the circles were inseparable. You understand?"

We nodded hurriedly, anxious for her to continue with the story.

"Unfortunately, things began to change quite soon after the formation of these circles. Tiny hairline cracks began to emerge in the alliances between fairies and humans. As more and more humans stopped believing in fairies, the cracks became chasms, which grew bigger and bigger, and eventually led to a complete parting of the ways. Within only a few hundred years, the friendships that had once existed between humans and fairies had vanished completely."

Daisy coughed pointedly. The fairy looked at her. "*Almost* completely," she said with a smile.

"So what happened to the portals?" I asked.

"The portals didn't go anywhere," Chara went on. "Nor did their use change. They were still gateways between the two worlds. The only difference was that humans no longer knew — or cared — how to use them. To humans, fairies were the stuff of children's stories. They no longer believed, and with this disbelief came the denial of our existence, so we became invisible."

"Invisible to humans?" I asked.

Chara nodded. "To *most* humans. Of course, over the years there have still been those who have believed—usually children—and they have had a sighting or two. But beyond that, it's been as though we don't exist."

"So what happened then?" Daisy asked. "If we weren't friends with humans anymore, why did we still need the portals?"

"Just because humans no longer believed in us, this didn't mean that our role in their lives changed. We still continued to visit their world, to do whatever we could to protect and look after them."

"But why would you do that?" I asked. "If humans denied that you even existed, why keep on helping them—I mean, us?"

Chara smiled. "Because, my dear, we need one another."

"But why? I mean, it's obvious we need *you*. You do so much for us, like deliver our dreams and help us if something really bad happens! But why do you need *us*?"

"Have you ever noticed what we are—a rain cloud, a flower, butterfly? We *are* a part of the earth. That's where we get our magic. We look after humans.

Humans look after the planet — or so we hope. Humans might have forgotten about our existence, but it doesn't change the fact that we need one another in order to survive."

"So, go on," Daisy said. "Tell us what happened with the portals."

"Each portal has a fairy to operate it," Chara went on. "We call them the stone fairies, because they govern and control the portal stones, infusing them with fairy power so that the portals continue to operate. And the portals are all connected, so that if one ceases to work, gradually they will all break down and fail. Each of the stone fairies stays at his or her post for a hundred years."

"A hundred years?" I broke in. "Wow!"

"It is a long time, yes. One of the longest of any of ATC's assignments. These fairies are among the most important fairies in the whole of the FG world. Without them, the portals wouldn't function, and the links between the two worlds would be closed up forever."

"OK," Daisy said. "But we still don't see why —"

"The stone fairy at the Tidehill Rocks portal is missing," Alya broke in.

No one said anything for a while. After a few moments, I found my voice. "Missing?" I said. "How can a fairy be missing?"

"We don't know exactly how she disappeared," Chara said. "Since the portals aren't used much anymore, we don't keep a close eye on their activities. This particular stone fairy is about three quarters of the way through her assignment. All we know is that she disappeared on a misty night a week and a half ago."

"A week and a half?" Daisy broke in. "But we've used it since then. I thought the portal couldn't operate without the stone fairy."

"It can't for long," Chara said. "Since all of the portals are connected, it can draw magic from the stone fairies at the other portals, but only for a short while. The stone fairies belong to a very special FG department, whose sole role is the movement between the human and fairy worlds."

"That's NMD, isn't it?" Daisy said.

"It is indeed."

"NMD — what's that?" I asked.

Daisy turned to me. "New Moon Department. It's one of the most secret departments. No one knows much about it except that it controls access between the human and fairy worlds."

"Well, you are about to be among the few who know more than that," Chara went on. "The way these portals work is linked with the cycle of the moon. Each new moon infuses the stone fairy with the power to do his or her job and keep the portal working. This fairy's disappearance means that the portal can only continue to operate for the rest of the current moon's cycle. After that, if we have not found her and restored her to the portal stone, then the portal will close. And trust us, this would be disastrous — for humans and fairies alike."

"So why do you need us?" I asked. "How can we help you find the stone fairy?"

"The fairy transforms on Earth as a gemstone. In this case, her name is Amber, as that is what form she takes. As a piece of amber, she was kept well out of sight at the top of the highest stone. There is magic built into the formation of the stones purely to protect their fairy. It states that if the stone fairy is ever removed from the circle, she will be kept in a safe place that can only be reached by a human and fairy together. A very special place."

"How special?" I asked.

"As magical as a hole in time," Chara replied.

"A whole what?" I asked.

"A hole in time," she repeated. "The moment the fairy leaves the circle, a small tear in time opens up and she slips through it. She is kept safe on the other side, in a place where time is frozen at the exact moment that she left the circle."

I stared hard at Chara, wondering if at some point someone was going to jump out and tell me this whole thing was one big joke.

"I still don't see how we fit in," Daisy said.

"Since this portal was made to connect the fairy and human worlds, in order to protect it from anyone who may not have good intentions, only a fairy and human pair with a strong bond can travel together freely to and from this special place. The human and fairy have to have a friendship worthy of the portal's magic," Chara replied. "A type of friendship that was once commonplace, but which is now virtually nonexistent."

"A friendship that could pass the highest loyalty test," Alya continued. Then she paused and looked slowly from Daisy to me and back again.

"A friendship like ours," Daisy said.

"Without this friendship, a human or a fairy can get *into* the place of safety, but cannot get out again," Alya went on. "This rule was sealed into the magic of the stones — so that if a day ever came when either fairy or human tried to steal the portal's magic, they could not get far. As soon as the stone fairy is taken outside of the circle, she is transported to this place, and her captor is transported there too. They will both remain trapped there until the human and fairy pair retrieve them. Then the stone fairy will be brought back to the circle to fulfill her assignment. And the person who has stolen her has a choice — come back with her and face punishment for the crime —"

"Or be stuck wandering around forever in a place where everything except for them is frozen in time," I finished.

Alya smiled at me. "You are a quick learner," she said.

Chara continued. "The commitment of friendship was part of the magic," she said. "If the day came when the stone fairy was removed and such friendships no longer existed, it would be impossible to get her back. Humans and fairies agreed that if this day ever came, the portals would no longer *need* to work; they figured the two worlds could part company forever if that were the case. But they failed to see what the long-term implications of that would be."

"So the stone fairy would be trapped in that place?" Daisy asked.

Chara looked at Daisy. "As you know, all fairy godmothers take their assignments very seriously," she said. "And none more than the stone fairies," she went on. "When a stone fairy is appointed, she makes a solemn promise of commitment to the stone circle — and to the fairy godmother world. She is given one of the most important tasks there is, to maintain the link between the two worlds, and in exchange she agrees to give her power to the portal."

"I don't understand," I said. "What power does she give the portal?"

"The power to transport," Chara said. "In order to permit the fairies, or humans, to move between the two worlds, the stone fairy gives up her power to do the same."

"A fairy can do that?"

"Absolutely," Chara said. "Any fairy who is willing to make such a sacrifice is special and powerful enough to do this. By promising to give the circle her power, her magic and the circle's become one and the same."

"And even with all this, you would still agree to abandon her to the land of frozen time if things went wrong? After everything she'd sacrificed?" I asked.

Chara looked at me. "You must remember, the portals were built in very different times from these. No one imagined that such a day would *ever* come."

I let out a breath that I felt I'd been holding for the whole conversation. It was just so much to take in. "And you're absolutely sure about all this?" I asked.

Alya clicked her fingers and the room went dark. Behind her, a bright white wall appeared with a slight crackling sound, like an old movie was running. And then the pictures appeared on the wall.

"These are the latest image predictions from EDD," she said.

"What's EDD?" I whispered to Daisy.

"You don't want to know!" she whispered back.

"Daisy!" I whispered again, more insistently. "Tell me!"

"Emergencies, Disasters, and Doom," she said reluctantly. "You *don't* ignore a prediction from them."

"As you can see," Alya was saying over hundreds of images of stone circles losing their color, then crumbling and becoming circles of dust in the ground, "the first thing that happens is that the portal's breakdown spreads to all the other portals." The picture changed to an image of a rainbow, then another, and another, until the screen was filled with rainbows. Then in between the rainbows came pictures of rays of sun and shooting stars — and then every single one disappeared, turned to gray, dissolved into dust like the stone circles.

"The breakdown will soon spread to all other methods of transportation and communication until fairies have no interaction at all with the human world," Alya said. "Initially, the consequences would be relatively minor. A little less color in the world, a little less light. A few tears falling without being caught, a few wishes unanswered. And of course — no more dreams. Do you know how much people value their dreams?"

I shook my head.

"Enough to make them desperate for sleep. EDD has shown us that people's sleeping patterns can go haywire just so they can have a dream! The tiredness alone will lead to many accidents." She snapped her fingers, and a new screen came up. People slumped over desks, falling asleep in their cars, on buses, out walking their dogs. There was even one of a pilot falling asleep while flying a plane!

"There will be many accidents, more and more all the time. And with no MTB to determine which disasters can be prevented, and no SRB to help people cope with the terrible things that are unavoidable, the world will soon be in complete disarray."

She showed more pictures: scenes of disaster, each one more devastating than the last. Multiple car pileups, houses on fire, fights in the streets — all set against a world that became grayer and duller with every picture.

"And of course, there is nature itself," Alya said somberly. "If fairies are unable to visit Earth, everything that lives and grows will eventually die out completely." She snapped her fingers once more. "This is EDD's prediction for the world in just a hundred years."

The last picture was the most shocking of them all. There were no trees. No plants. Hardly an animal. The shot scanned the face of the planet and found nothing but desert.

Alya snapped her fingers, and the screen went black. The four of us sat in the darkness in silence.

I cleared my throat. "So let me get this right," I said shakily. "Daisy and I have to go to the portal, somehow get through a hole in time, find the stone fairy, and bring her back."

"Correct," Alya said.

"And we have to do this before the next new moon, because the portal can only keep working for the rest of this moon's cycle."

"That's right."

"And if we don't succeed, this"—I pointed to the now blank screen—"is EDD's prediction for the future?"

The fairy nodded.

"And what about us?" I asked. "If we get in there, but don't get back out in time, what happens to us?"

Alya cleared her throat. Chara looked away.

"What?" Daisy asked.

"When the new moon rises, the hole in time is sealed," she said.

"What does that mean?" I asked.

"It means . . ." Chara began. Then she stopped.

Alya continued for her. "It means . . ." She paused. Then she looked slowly from Daisy to me and back again. "It means you would be stuck there forever."

I stared at her. Could she really be asking this of us? Was there *honestly* any way in the world we could possibly take on such a task when the stakes were so high? Then I thought about the pictures. Could we really *not* do it?

"When is the next new moon due to rise?" Daisy asked.

"Just after midnight on New Year's Eve."

"New Year's Eve!" I blurted out. "You're kidding! That's tonight!"

"Exactly," Alya said. "Now you understand the urgency and the importance of this task."

I tried to take in what they were saying. It was impossible! It was crazy! There was no *way* we could take on such an enormous task.

I was about to open my mouth to say so, but Daisy spoke first. "We do understand," she said, "and we are honored that you've asked us." And then, with a brief look at me, and clearly misunderstanding my stunned silence for agreement, she added, "We'll do it."

chapter ten

Philippa

"Let's get to work," Alya said.

I opened my mouth to protest. Did they realize
what they were asking of us? But each time I was
about to say something, to tell them they'd made a
mistake and I wasn't going to do it, I thought of those
images they'd shown us. It was so hard to believe.
But it was true. Those things *would* happen —
and only Daisy and I could stop them.

I shut my mouth again and listened.

"You have to go to the portal, but one of you
needs to be on each side of the divide for it to work.
Daisy here, Philippa back on Earth. Then you —"

"I get to go back to Earth?" I broke in. "Really?"

"You have to approach the hole in time from both sides of the divide at the same time — one from the human world and one from the fairy side," Chara said. "It's the only way."

"But — I mean, that's great!" I said. "I can go back to Earth!"

Alya shifted awkwardly in her seat.

"What?" I asked.

"Philippa, you realize that you are going back to Earth for one reason only: to get through the hole in time, fetch the stone fairy, and bring her back to her place in the portal."

"I know, but . . ."

My voice trailed away. Again, those horrible images came into my head. Set against the kind of things EDD had predicted, my personal traumas seemed petty, and saying out loud how much I wanted to see my parents and Robyn would only sound selfish.

Alya smiled. "At the end of all this, you can go back to Earth for good. For now you have a job to do. But if we're right about all of this, it should go smoothly. Now that we've found you, we can all relax a bit."

Relax a bit? Did she *really* just say that? They were about to send Daisy and me on a mission where we could end up being stuck forever in a place where time had frozen, while the world turned into a big desert, and she was talking about *relaxing*?

Alya must have read my thoughts because she quickly went on. "Obviously, when I say 'relax,' I don't mean it in the traditional sense. But it *should* be straightforward enough. All you have to do is get through the hole, grab the stone fairy, and bring her back. She should be waiting for you on the other side, in her stone form, a piece of amber."

"What makes you so sure of this?" I asked.

"We've tried to contact her via her MagiCell, but haven't managed to get through. We're fairly sure this means that she hasn't transformed." Alya shuffled uncomfortably.

"What aren't you telling us?" Daisy asked.

"We're not positive about this," Alya said. "It could mean that it's impossible to make MagiCell contact within the hole in time."

"We have never had the occasion to try it before," Chara added. "That's why we need you. But remember — she's a fairy godmother, and she has an important job, so we can safely assume that she will be waiting to get back to it."

"But what if she isn't?" I asked. "I mean, we still don't know how she got there. If someone stole her, they won't *want* her to be returned or maybe they've taken her somewhere else." A shiver of fear slithered through me as I imagined armed gangs on the other side, refusing to give us the stone fairy and willing to fight us for her.

"You're right," Alya said calmly. "We don't know how she got there. And yes, we must assume that somebody stole her."

"So what about them — the person, or people, who took her?" I asked. "Do we leave them there?"

"Our concern is the stone fairy," Alya replied. "She will be waiting for you on the other side of the hole, and you *must* bring her back. But if you find the thief, he or she should be brought back too. If necessary, the thief will be punished."

"Punished?" I asked. "What kind of punishment?"

"We will determine that at the time, when we know all the circumstances," Chara said. "You don't need to worry about that now. All you need to do is hold the stone fairy in between the two of you — and the thief, if appropriate — and bring them back through the hole in time with you."

I let out a breath. This really wasn't the kind of thing you imagined getting caught up in when you went to visit your friend for a relaxing vacation. My friend, Robyn — who knew nothing about any of this — was probably down there on Earth worried sick about us both.

"I want to see my parents and Robyn," I said.

"There's no time," Alya said. "You have to go through the hole at the exact same time of day that it first opened up."

"What time was that?" I asked.

"Four minutes and seventeen seconds past five in the evening," Alya replied.

Wow, she wasn't joking when she said exact. I checked my watch. "We've got four hours," I said.

"We have to get you both prepared, make all the necessary arrangements. It simply can't be —"

"I at least need to see Robyn," I said. "She's in this with us. I'm not going to just abandon her — especially if there's a chance that I'm never coming back from this!"

The fairies exchanged a glance. "Philippa, this isn't good-bye. It will all be fine," Chara said.

"You can't guarantee that," I said. "*Please.*"

Alya let out a breath and shook her head. "OK. Here's how it'll work," she said. "You can see Robyn on two conditions."

"What are the conditions?"

"One, you have to be quick. You see her, say what you have to say, and then come straight to the portal to begin the assignment."

"OK," I said. "What's the other?"

"Under no circumstances do you tell her *anything* about what you're doing for us. This assignment must be kept absolutely between us. It has been given the highest level of confidentiality."

"Why?" Daisy asked.

"Can you imagine what would happen if word got out?" Chara said. "The panic at ATC alone could destroy everything, never mind if anyone on Earth heard about it. The rumors would be devastating. So you can see your friend for a few minutes, but not a word about your assignment. Agreed?"

"Agreed," I said.

"Good. And when this is all over," Chara went on, "you will be returned to Earth and can get back to your normal life."

And then, before I even had the chance to jump in the air and scream "Woohoo," we were dismissed.

"Go, now," Chara said. "Our assistants will help you prepare for your assignment. And girls — be careful."

"We will," Daisy said. "You can trust us."

"We know that," Alya said with a smile. "It's why we chose you."

Robyn

What was that?

I was in my bedroom, sitting beside the radiator on my beanbag chair reading a magazine when something hit the window behind me.

I jumped up and looked out the window. Nothing there. I snuggled back into the beanbag and had just started reading my magazine again when I heard it once more.

Tap.

Something was hitting the window. I got up and peered outside again, looking all over to see what it was. That was when I saw her. She was hiding behind a row of garbage cans across the road. Philippa!

Or was it Daisy, transformed as Philippa? Either way, she was beckoning me to come outside.

I ran down the stairs and through the shop. "Just going out for a minute," I said to Dad, and was out of the door before he had a chance to reply.

"Daisy?" I said uncertainly as I crept around the back of the cans.

She stepped out and grinned at me. "It's me — Philippa!" she said.

"Philippa! It's actually, really you?"

She laughed. "Yes, it's me!"

"I can't believe it," I said. "I'm so glad to see you!" I glanced around at the trash cans in the alley. "Why here?" I asked. "Why didn't you just come in?"

"I can't let anyone else see me. I don't have very long," she said. "I begged them to let me see you before —" She stopped and blushed.

"Before what?" I asked.

Philippa shook her head. "I can't tell you. It's one of the conditions of ATC letting me see you. I wanted to know how you're doing."

"How are *you* doing?" I asked. "And Daisy. Is she OK? Did she get into terrible trouble? Have they found you out yet? How come you're here, anyway?"

Philippa laughed. "Too many questions. I haven't got time to answer them all now."

"Oh," I said. "Well, can I at least ask where you're going?"

Philippa looked at me seriously. "Listen, I've just got to do something with Daisy, but it'll all be over by tonight."

I bit my tongue to stop asking more questions. They were only stupid, jealous questions anyway. Like whether she preferred doing things with Daisy, and if Daisy was more fun, being a fairy godsister and all that. How could I ever compete with her?

"I can't wait to celebrate New Year's with you tonight," Philippa said, reading my mind so perfectly that I felt instantly guilty for all my silly worries. "No matter what happens, I'll be back in time for the fireworks."

"Promise?" I asked.

"Promise," Philippa said, although the way she wouldn't meet my eyes made me wonder how sure she was that she'd get back safely from whatever she had to do. "All you need to know is that I'm OK, Daisy's OK, no one's been punished, and as long as everything goes according to plan, life will be back to normal again by tonight."

I smiled. "OK," I said, forcing myself not to focus on the "as long as everything goes according to plan" part.

Philippa glanced at her watch. "Listen, I have to go," she said.

"Is there any way I can keep in touch with you?" I asked. "Any way of sending me a message, just to let me know you're OK?"

Philippa shook her head. But then she stopped. "Wait!" She reached into her pocket. "Take this."

She handed me something that looked kind of like a cell phone. "Is that a phone?" I asked. "But I've already got —"

"It's not a normal phone; it's a MagiCell," she said. "They gave it to me at ALD."

"They what?"

Philippa shook her head. "Look, it doesn't matter. Just keep it. We'll have Daisy's. I don't know if it'll work on the other —" She stopped and clapped a hand over her mouth. "In the place we're going," she said quietly. "But if it does, we'll try to contact you."

I held the MagiCell tightly in my hand. "I won't let it out of my sight," I said.

Philippa smiled. "Good. We'll contact you if we can," she said. "I'd better go. See you later."

"Yeah, see you later," I replied. And only when she'd run to the end of the street and rounded the corner did I whisper, "Good luck."

chapter eleven

Philippa

It was nearly five o'clock. I made my way to the stone circle, making sure to follow the path. I couldn't risk any mistakes at this stage!

By this time, the light of day had all but gone — the colors were shutting down, replaced by various combinations of gray.

At the right moment, I had to stand in the center of the circle and turn around three times.

I looked around to make sure no one else was here. Thankfully, the place was deserted. I checked my watch. Three minutes past five. I waited in the center of the circle. Four minutes past. My heart thudded hard in my chest. Ten seconds, fifteen, seventeen. This was it. I stretched out my arms and turned slowly around, praying that Daisy was doing exactly the same on the other side.

Around once, around twice. A third time, and then—

The stone circle disappeared. I was enveloped in a pitch-black void. There was nothing here—nothing in the whole of space except me, spinning slowly around, waiting for something to come and take me to the place of frozen time.

Daisy! Daisy! Where are you?

Something was emerging out of the darkness.

"Daisy?" I called uncertainly.

The something emerged into a person. It was her!

"Philippa! You made it!" she said, smiling at me across the darkness.

"So did you!" I said, letting out a huge breath of relief.

"You ready?" she asked.

"I think so."

"Come on, let's go," she said.

I held out my arms and crossed them over, as High Command had told us. Daisy did the same, and we took hold of each other's hands.

"OK?" Daisy asked. I went over the rhyme in my head. The one the fairies had told us to memorize — the one that would only work if our bond was strong enough. This was the point where we would find out the true value of our friendship.

I nodded, and we recited the rhyme together.

> *Cross your arms and link your hands*
> *And say aloud this rhyme.*
> *Then travel through the portal*
> *To the place of frozen time.*

We finished the rhyme and looked at each other. And then, a moment later, I looked up and saw a streak of light heading toward us like a dart. The light flew right at us, hitting us both and lighting up a bright white circle that enclosed us.

It had worked!

The circle turned from white into every color you could imagine, until it felt as if we were in the center of a circular rainbow.

I turned around, staring at the colors dancing and popping around us, spinning and growing from the rainbow's circle into a ball, enveloping us almost completely. It felt as though the colors were spin-ning a web — with us enclosed on the inside.

The colors kept growing and extending and mul-tiplying until — suddenly — they stopped. They had joined at every point. We were completely con-tained in a dancing, flashing ball of colors.

I had to shield my eyes from the brightness. "Is this supposed to happen?" I asked nervously.

"I imagine so," Daisy replied. Then she pointed behind me. "Look!" she gasped.

I turned around. Among the dancing lights and colors, a tiny black hole was opening up. It started about as large as my eye, but grew and grew until it was the size of a basketball.

"That's it," Daisy said, pulling me over to the hole. "We have to go through there."

The hole was probably *just* big enough to crawl though. I suddenly remembered I'd always been a little afraid of small spaces. It didn't seem like a good time to mention this to Daisy, so I did the only thing I could do. I took the biggest breath I could — and followed her into the hole.

* * *

We crawled along the tunnel for a few minutes, and then it started going upward, getting steeper and steeper, until eventually we had to grip the sides and pull ourselves on.

"Daisy, look!" I pointed above us. There was a grayish light ahead. Only slightly lighter than the blackness of the hole, but it looked different.

We clambered and heaved and pulled ourselves up higher and higher until, finally, the grayish light was directly above us. Daisy was ahead of me. She dragged herself up through the top of the hole and reached down to help me through. I held on to her hand and pulled myself up. The second I was through it, the hole started to shrink. Smaller and smaller, down to the size of a quarter, a penny, a dot. And then it disappeared altogether. It was as though it had never been there.

Standing next to Daisy, I tore my eyes away from the ground and looked around. I could hardly believe what I was seeing.

"The stone circle," Daisy breathed.

"On the evening the stone fairy disappeared," I added. The sky was gray, just as it had been when I left, the fading light of a winter's afternoon. I looked at my watch. It had frozen on the time I'd come through the hole. From now on, only Daisy's MagiCell would give us the right time. Here, it would be just after five o'clock all day.

I looked into the sky and gasped. "Daisy, look," I said in a whisper, pointing at a bird that was hovering absolutely stock-still, directly above us. It had stopped in the middle of flapping its wings upward.

"Whoa, that is weird," Daisy said. The more I looked around, the more birds I saw, caught like a photograph, midflight.

It was eerie. There was no movement at all. No wind. No sounds. Everything was completely, utterly, totally still.

"Frozen solid, all of it," I said. "At least we know we're in the right place!"

Daisy nodded and looked around. "Now all we need to do is find the stone fairy."

We walked around the stone circle, assuming she would be somewhere just on the outside of it, like the High Command fairies had told us. They'd said she should still be in stone form as a piece of amber. But there was a small possibility she could have transformed. If so, she could be anything! All we knew for sure was that the stone fairy would be the only thing around here that wasn't frozen in time.

Well, the stone fairy and whoever had stolen her.

I shuddered and walked around the circle again.

"She's not here," I said as I met up with Daisy on the other side.

"I think you're right," she said. "But that's . . ." Her voice trailed off.

"That's what?" I asked, but Daisy just shook her head.

"Should we look farther afield?" I asked, glancing at the miles and miles of forest surrounding us and wondering where on earth to start.

Daisy was pressing buttons on her MagiCell. "Give me a minute," she said. "I've had a thought."

I waited a minute while Daisy pressed more buttons. "I don't understand," she said. "It should be working."

"Daisy, what are you trying to do?" I asked.

She turned to me. "Look, all fairies have Magi-Cells for their assignments, right?"

"Right," I agreed.

"When you're in Nature Mode it doesn't materialize with you."

"Nature Mode?" I asked.

"You know. The form that you take for your assignment. Like I was a daisy when I gave you three wishes, and then I was a butterfly when I was working with Dream Delivery Department. I only had my MagiCell when I transformed back to a fairy or a human."

"OK," I said. "So when the stone fairy is a piece of amber, she won't have her MagiCell, but if she transformed when she got here, she should have it?"

"Exactly," Daisy said. "And she must have transformed, or else we'd see the amber lying around nearby."

"So what are you trying to do?" I asked.

"Well, if she *has* transformed, her MagiCell will have materialized, and I should be able to get a reading of where she is."

"High Command couldn't get through to her, though, remember?"

"I know," Daisy said distractedly. "They thought it was because she hadn't transformed, but perhaps it was because they couldn't communicate across the divide. In which case, we should be able to contact her from here."

"And?" I asked hopefully. "Have you got anything yet?"

Daisy shook her head. "Nothing—except this." Daisy held out her MagiCell. "Listen."

I held it to my ear. Screeching and crackling sounds whirred away through the speaker. "Ouch," I said, holding the MagiCell away from my ear.

"I just don't get it. It should work. Unless . . ."

"Unless her MagiCell hasn't materialized and she's still a piece of amber," I said.

"Exactly."

"But then she should be here." I looked helplessly around again.

"Unless the thief has taken her somewhere," Daisy said.

"Oh," I said. "In which case she could be absolutely anywhere!" Now what? This was starting to feel like a whole different assignment from the apparently quick and simple one the fairies at High Command had described.

Daisy had taken the MagiCell back and was pressing buttons again.

"What are you doing?" I asked.

"I'm going to contact High Command," she said. "We'll have to tell them what's going on."

"What, tell them we've failed already? How's that going to look when they've put their faith in us to do this? You heard what they said. We're the best hope they've got — their *only* hope! We can't tell them we've let them down — not yet. They'll panic if they know their only option has failed."

Daisy stopped punching buttons. "Have you got any better ideas?"

I opened my mouth to reply. I was about to say no. Of *course* I didn't have any ideas. If Daisy didn't know how to get us out of this, there wasn't much chance that *I* did!

But then I had a thought. "Wait! Actually, yes, I have got an idea," I said. "Why don't we go down to the village and see if we can find a local paper or something, or get online? We know exactly when the stone fairy disappeared, and we're pretty sure someone stole her. Maybe there'll be something in the news or on the Internet about someone disappearing?"

Daisy stared at me. "Philippa, aren't you forgetting something?" she asked in the kind of voice that you use when you're talking to someone very slow on the uptake, but you're trying to be kind about it.

I stared back at her. What had I forgotten?

"The second the stone fairy came here, time stood still," Daisy said. "There won't be anything in any newspapers, because no newspapers have come out here since it happened! And the computers will be frozen in time, just like those birds. Over here, it's the exact same moment as it was when the stone fairy disappeared!"

Oh, yes. *That* was what I'd forgotten.

"And anyway, there's not much chance of the newspapers reporting that a piece of amber no one knew existed has disappeared from a group of stones that hardly anyone ever visits!"

"No! But the thief will have disappeared, too. And somebody must have noticed *that*! Think about it — someone must be missing their mom or dad or brother or sister. They might be trying to find them."

Daisy rubbed her lip. "You're right. But we've still got no way of getting that information. We're going to be really limited in what we can find here. The only things with any life in them around here are going to be the stone fairy herself, the person who stole her, and you and me."

"And the MagiCell!" I said, suddenly brightening up as I had a new thought. Of course! "Daisy, you know how you're trying to contact the stone fairy's MagiCell?"

"Er, yes," Daisy said uncertainly. "And it's not working."

"But you think you can still contact other Magi-Cells from yours, right?" I asked.

"Yes, but I thought you didn't want to get in touch with ATC yet."

"I'm not talking about contacting ATC," I said.

"Well, what are you —"

"Contact me!" I burst out. "Contact my MagiCell! The one your supervisor gave me!"

Daisy looked at me as though I'd gone crazy. "Philippa, you're right here, beside me. What's the point of me contacting *you*?"

"I don't have it!" I said. "Robyn does!"

Daisy frowned, pursing her lips together and squinting at me as she tried to catch up with my thinking. Was she angry?

"I gave it to her so we could keep in touch. She might be able to help us," I said.

Daisy looked at me blankly.

"Look. We know what day the stone fairy disappeared. We even know exactly what time. And we're pretty sure someone stole her, right?"

"Right," Daisy agreed.

"And we know that we can't get access to any of that information here, since there won't be any newspapers since it happened, and all the computers will almost certainly also be frozen."

"Ye-e-s."

"Well, maybe there *is* something about it online."

"But I've already told you, we can't. They'll be —"

"Not us — Robyn!"

Daisy stared at me. And then, finally, I saw her eyes brighten as though someone had switched a light on inside them. "Of course!" she said. "We contact Robyn and get her to go online and see what she can find! Philippa, it's brilliant!"

I felt my cheeks redden as I smiled at Daisy. "Well, I don't know if it's brilliant," I said, "but it's got to be worth a try."

Robyn

I looked at my watch for the thousandth time. Nearly six o'clock. Where were Philippa and Daisy? What were they doing? Were they in danger?

I couldn't concentrate on anything except the questions that chased each other around and around in my head — none of which had any answers.

I grabbed the magazine I'd been reading, but I couldn't concentrate on a word. Just as I was attempting to read the same article for the tenth time, I heard a buzzing noise on the other side of my room.

What was that? It wasn't my cell phone. A few weeks ago, Dad had decided we needed to get into the Christmas spirit and had changed my ringtone to "Jingle Bells"!

Was it an alarm of some sort?

I put the magazine down and went to investigate.

It seemed to be coming from underneath my bean-bag chair. Wait—that was where I'd been sitting when I was last holding . . .

Philippa's MagiCell!

I grabbed the MagiCell. How did you work one of these things? Why hadn't I thought to ask?

I pressed frantically at every button that looked as if it might do something until, eventually, I heard a loud crackle, followed by . . .

"Hello?"

Philippa! I gripped the MagiCell tighter and spoke into it. "Philippa, is that you?" I asked.

"Robyn! It's working!" She sounded fuzzy and crackly and distant, and I couldn't make out the words all that clearly, but it was her! I'd never been so relieved to hear anyone's voice!

"Where are you?" I asked. "It's a really bad connection. Are you out in the middle of nowhere?"

Philippa snorted. "You could say that," she said. "Listen, we haven't got much time. I need to ask you a favor."

"Anything! What do you want?"

"We need information about something that happened ten days ago. That's Tuesday of last week."

"OK, what is it? What happened?"

There was a long pause.

"Philippa, are you still there?"

"Yeah, I'm still here," she said. "The thing is, we don't *know* what happened. That's what we need to find out."

"Huh? You need information about something, but you don't know what you need information about?"

"Something happened last Tuesday," she went on. "We don't know exactly what it was, but we think someone might be missing."

"Someone's disappeared? Who?"

"That's just it — we don't know!"

"Can't ATC find out?"

"Hang on," Philippa said. "I'm putting Daisy on."

Another pause, then I heard Daisy's voice. "Hi, Robyn," she said.

"Daisy?"

"Yes. Listen, I know this won't make much sense to you. We're not at ATC at the moment. They might have been able to find this person earlier, but they didn't think they'd need to. They weren't particularly interested in finding the human, just the —" She broke off. "Listen, it doesn't matter. We just need to find them now."

"OK, well, do you know where they live?"

"Probably in your village, or somewhere nearby."

"You can't give me anything more than that to go on?"

"I'm sorry. We're *really* not allowed to say anything. We shouldn't even be contacting you, but we can't think of any other way of getting the information without making things worse."

"OK, I understand," I said. Which wasn't exactly true. I mean, how could I understand when they could only tell me half of the story — and the half they *could* tell me didn't make sense? Either way, I did know one thing: if Philippa and Daisy needed help, there was no way I was going to say no. "Just tell me what you need me to do," I said.

"Get hold of any local newspapers that came out since last Tuesday, and try online, too. See if there's any mention of someone missing. Or anything out of the ordinary that happened at around that time — possibly near Tidehill Rocks. Can you do that?"

"Of course I can," I said, crossing over to my desk and switching my computer on. "I'll get on it now."

"Great. OK, we'll see what else we can find out here. If you get anything, press the button you pressed to answer this call and then type my name into the MagiCell. It should put you through to us."

"What, just type *Daisy*?" I asked.

"No! My real name. FG32561."

"Wait!" I grabbed a pencil and some paper from my desk. "OK, tell me again."

"FG32561," Daisy repeated. I scribbled it down. "Call as soon as you have anything."

"I will," I said. "Good luck."

"Thanks," Daisy replied. And as my computer whirred to life and connected to the Internet, she added in a quieter voice, "We'll need it."

chapter twelve

Philippa

We walked around the village looking for clues and trying not to be too freaked out by the frozen time thing going on all around us. It was like being in a horror movie. Everywhere we looked, people were rooted to the spot like statues.

There was a man in the process of getting up from a bench. He was balanced halfway between sitting and standing in what looked like an impossible semicrouch. I couldn't help thinking his knees would ache for a week once he got out of that position. A young couple was poised at the edge of a sidewalk, holding hands and each sticking a foot out into the road. Coming toward them, farther down the road, a bus was frozen with about twenty statue-like passengers. Some of them were looking at each other openmouthed, in the middle of a conversation; others stared out the window with various expressions of boredom and impatience stamped solid on their faces.

"This is spooky," I whispered. I probably didn't need to whisper. I mean, it wasn't as if anyone could hear us or see us, or even as if they knew we were there. But the silence and eeriness of it all made me nervous.

"Look," Daisy said as we turned a corner onto a new street. A statue dog was perched with his leg up in the air, obviously about to christen the lamppost beside him. I laughed.

"OK," Daisy said. "We've been here over an hour already, and we still haven't found the stone fairy. We're just wandering around the town with no idea where to look."

Daisy's MagiCell beeped before I had a chance to reply. She grabbed it and looked at the screen. "It's Robyn!"

"Can you put her on speakerphone?"

Daisy pressed a few buttons, and a moment later I heard Robyn's voice.

"How are you doing?" she asked.

"Not great," Daisy said. "We don't know where to start. What about you? Have you got anything for us?"

"I think so. I couldn't find anything on the Internet," Robyn said. "I put in the day, the date, and the place, but nothing came up. I've tried all sorts of variations."

"And?" I asked. "Then what? You said you've got something."

"Well, then I went to the newsstands," she went on. "Mrs. Crowther always keeps at least one copy of each week's local papers. She makes an annual scrapbook out of them. Anyway, I searched through last week's and —"

"Robyn, what have you found?" I snapped impatiently.

"It's a boy," she said. "He disappeared — last Tuesday."

"A boy?" I repeated. "Our thief is a kid?"

"Your what?"

Daisy shook her head at me. "Nothing," she replied. "Tell us more about this boy."

"He's twelve, his name is Tommy, and he lives on Greenacre Lane. In fact, as soon as I read about it, I realized it sounded familiar. Some of the locals were talking about a missing boy at the shop last week, but I hadn't thought anything of it at the time. Apparently, his parents hadn't wanted to do interviews or anything—they were hoping he'd turn up at any moment."

"But he hasn't?" I asked.

"No," Robyn replied. "Not as far as I know."

Daisy was punching numbers into her MagiCell.

"Greenacre Lane?" she asked. The screen brought up a map of where we were. There was a blue line that led from us to Greenacre Lane. "It's not far away," Daisy said. "Probably about a mile."

"I don't know what number," Robyn went on. "It's just got the road."

"OK," I said. "Let's go."

But Robyn stopped me. "Is he in trouble?" she asked. "I mean—if you find him, will anything bad happen to him? Just, well, he's only twelve. The article says his parents are out of their minds with worry."

"He's not going to be in trouble," I said with a glance at Daisy. She quickly turned away from me, and I wasn't so sure I was right. But Robyn didn't need to know that. She had enough to worry about already.

"I'm not even sure he's going to be the right person," Robyn went on. "The paper came out on Wednesday; he might have been found since then. But he's all I've got."

"You've done a fantastic job," Daisy said. "Thank you so much."

"It's OK," Robyn said. "I just hope it helps."

"Listen, we need to go," Daisy said.

"We'll get in touch again," I added. "Don't worry about us, OK?"

"OK," Robyn agreed. Her quaking voice sounded about as unworried as mine.

We got to Greenacre Lane and looked all down the street. There were about twenty houses on each side.

"Where do we start?" I asked.

Daisy pointed across the road. "You take that side; I'll take this side. Call if you find anything, and I'll do the same."

I set off across the road and made my way up the first driveway. But when I got to the door, I stopped. What was I meant to do now? Break in? Rummage through a house that either had people frozen like statues, or a criminal inside?

I decided not to think about it.

"Hello?" I called, letting myself in to the screened porch. I tried the front door. It swung open! I guess people in small villages don't bother locking their doors in the daytime — luckily for us.

The house was silent.

"Hello?" I called again, a little more uncertainly this time as I crept through the hallway toward the kitchen.

Slowly opening the kitchen door, I took a step into the room and peered around. It was only when I looked beyond into the dining area that I saw them — a whole family sitting down to eat. All with mouths open, probably all talking at once; each one stopped in the middle of a word, knives and forks held in the air with food speared on the ends of them.

I ran out of the house without even looking upstairs. I couldn't bring myself to do it. It was just too spooky.

I took a few deep breaths and moved on to the next house. It was a similar scene, except in this one there was a boy sitting in front of a computer game in one room while the rest of the family was in the kitchen.

By the third house, I was starting to get used to it. This time, the father was outside in his driveway, his car door wide open, briefcase in hand and a smile half formed on his lips. The fourth, fifth, and sixth houses were similar — families settling in after work and school, each held in suspended animation in the middle of their evening activity. It was as if I'd been given a free pass to a wax museum — and I didn't like it!

I saw Daisy coming out of a house at the same time as I was, and I called over to her. "Find anything?"

She shook her head. "Nothing. What about you?"

"Same," I said. "We've done nearly half of them already. Perhaps he's not in any of them. Perhaps he isn't even the right person. We could be on the wrong track altogether."

"Yeah, we could be," Daisy agreed. "But it's the only track we've got to go on. We can't give up now."

"I know. You're right," I said.

Daisy turned toward the next house on her side, and I went back to mine.

This one felt different. The first thing I noticed was that the door was locked. I tried pushing my weight against it in case it was just stiff, but it didn't budge. Now what?

I noticed a path at the side of the house and followed it around to the backyard. The back door was one of those kind of stable doors with two halves.

The top half was locked, but it didn't seem to be properly joined to the bottom half. It was a rickety old door, and I guessed the joints were probably on the dad's list of things he'd get around to fixing one day. We have a long list of those — and none of them *ever* get done.

I pushed the bottom part of the door, and it moved a little — but it was jamming on something. Crouching down on the ground, I pressed my body against the door and heaved as hard as I could. Finally, it swung open, just enough for me to crawl through.

I crept through the opening on my hands and knees — and came face-to-face with an enormous dog with its jaws wide open, ready to eat me!

Clapping a hand over my mouth to stop myself from screaming, I told myself what I'd been repeating over and over again since we'd been doing this: *It's not going to harm you. It can't move. You're not in the middle of a zombie film. There's nothing to be scared of.*

Without taking my eyes off the dog, I squeezed past it and stood up. Once I'd done that, I realized it wasn't actually all that big. Still, I got through the back room as quickly as I could, and just to be on the safe side, I shut the door behind me.

I was in a kitchen. A woman was sitting at the table next to a baby in a high chair. The baby was looking up in the air with its mouth wide open; the woman was poised with her hand in the air holding a teaspoon as if it were an airplane about to come to land in the baby's mouth. I paused for a moment, remembering Dad telling me about doing the same thing with me. Only he would fly the airplane all around the room, and sometimes all over the house, before finally bringing it down to land in my mouth.

I opened the kitchen door and went out into the hallway.

And that was when the second different thing happened. I heard a noise.

My blood went as cold as if it had been taken out, replaced with some new blood straight out of the freezer, and siphoned back in again. Terror rooted my feet to the spot as firmly as if I had been frozen in time myself.

I tried to repeat my *there's nothing to be scared of* mantra, but it wouldn't work this time. Something about this house was different — I was sure of it.

I stood in my statue position in the hall, immobilized by indecision as much as fear. Should I go and get Daisy? Was it safe to tackle the thief on my own? If Robyn was right, he was only a twelve-year-old boy. But still, he *could* be a violent criminal. He could be a massive, burly, *scary* twelve-year-old boy.

I couldn't go and get Daisy. By the time I'd run across the road and back again, he'd probably have escaped — and then we'd have nothing.

I had to do this on my own.

I took a deep breath, clenched and unclenched my hands a few times, and crept up the stairs.

Tommy

What was *that*?

It was the first sound I'd heard in over a week. Nothing except me had moved, let alone made a sound, since I'd been trapped in this awful place.

I crept over to my bedroom door and listened through the crack. There it was again! It sounded like the floorboards at the bottom of the stairs. I knew those creaks inside and out from all the times I'd crept downstairs to sneak a cookie when I was supposed to be in bed.

Someone was in the house!

I looked around the room, desperately searching for a place to hide. Under the bed? No, too many smelly shoes and abandoned board games down there for me to fit.

Behind the curtains? No, too obvious.

Under my desk? Too exposed. I'd be seen right away.

"Hello?"

A voice! Someone was on the landing! My eyes felt as though they were about to pop out of their sockets, and my teeth started chattering so loudly I was convinced they'd give me away, no matter *where* I hid.

I heard the floorboard squeak right outside my door. That's the one I always have to do a big stretch to get over when I'm supposed to be in bed.

Too late to try and find a hiding place now. They'd be in my room in a second. I grabbed my bathrobe off the hook on the back of the door, pulled it over myself, and, for want of any better ideas, crouched down in a ball behind the door.

Philippa

"Hello?" I called again. Strange. I was sure I'd heard a noise earlier, but I'd been in almost every room and hadn't found anything, or anyone, yet.

I was at the last room. I'd have a quick check in here and then move on to the next house. I must have been mistaken about the noise. There was no one in the house. I'd probably imagined it because I'd been so freaked out by the dog.

I reached for the handle and pushed the door open.

And that was when the third different thing happened. Someone said, "Ouch."

I craned my neck around the door to see where the voice had come from. As far as I could tell, it had come from a bundle of clothes on the floor with a bathrobe on the top of it.

Taking a deep breath, I reached out with a shaking hand and lifted the bathrobe up.

"Don't hurt me! I'm sorry! Please don't hurt me!"

A boy was crouched on the floor, his hands over his head, his knees knocking together, and his words coming out in a terrified yelp.

"I'm not going to hurt you," I said as gently as I could.

"I haven't done anything; I don't know anything!" he yelped again. It suddenly occurred to me that I hadn't been expecting him to be even more frightened than I was. The only problem now was how to calm him down enough to try and get some sense out of him.

I crouched down next to him. "Look, it's OK. You're not in any trouble," I said in the most reassuring voice I could manage. I mean, I still didn't know exactly what trouble he *might* be in. I just knew I needed to calm him down and get him to help me find out what had happened to the stone fairy. Or, as far as he was concerned, to the piece of amber that he'd taken from the stone circle.

The boy lowered his hands from over his head. "Who are you?" he asked. "How did you get here? How come you're not frozen like everything else?"

"My name's Philippa," I said, trying to figure out how to answer the other questions and deciding that one out of three would have to do for now. "What's yours?"

"Tommy," he said. Tommy! He *was* the boy from the paper!

"How long have you been here, Tommy?" I asked.

"A — a week or two?" he said. "I don't know. Nothing works; nothing changes — you can't tell if it's day or night." His bottom lip began to tremble as he spoke. I could tell he was embarrassed; he turned his face away. I pretended I hadn't noticed. "It's been awful," he said, looking down into his lap. "It's like I'm the last person in the world. I don't know what happened; I don't know how I got here. I feel like I'm in one of those films where the world's been hit by an asteroid and there are only a few survivors. Except in my case, there's just me."

"And me," I said with a smile.

He looked at me. "Yeah, and you," he said. "Unless I'm just imagining you. I think I'm going crazy here. I've even started talking to myself. I keep thinking it must all be a bad dream. I keep going to sleep thinking that I'll wake up and things will be back to normal, but then I do wake up, and I'm still here on my own on this post-asteroid planet."

"What have you been eating?" I asked.

Tommy shrugged. "Canned food, cereal, lots of sandwiches. I'm starting to get sick of cold beans, to be honest."

"What about to drink?"

"I can get drinks out of bottles, but nothing comes out of the faucet. And no electricity or gas for cooking. No lights. No heating. Haven't you noticed it's *freezing*? Look!" He pointed to his bed. It had about five blankets piled up on it. "That's the only way I keep warm," he said. "I've taken them off all the other beds in the house." He turned to me. "What about you?" he asked. "How have you been surviving? Where did you come from? How did you find me, anyway?"

I took a breath. How was I going to explain it all to him?

"Listen, Tommy," I said. "I haven't been here as long as you. I knew you were here, and I've come to help you get back to your normal life."

"Really?" he breathed. "Can you do that? But how?"

"Well, I've got a friend with me. She's across the street at the moment. She's been looking for you, too. She'll help us," I said. "Listen, why don't you and I go and find her, and we'll take it from there?"

Tommy stood up. "OK," he said shakily. But he stopped at the door. "This isn't a trap, is it?" he asked. "You're not the bad guys, are you?" His face colored instantly, and I could tell he was ashamed to be sounding like such a scaredy cat — especially in front of a girl.

"I'm not bad at all," I reassured him. "And neither is Daisy."

We left the room and were halfway across the landing when I suddenly remembered the stone fairy.

"Oh, by the way, Tommy," I said, stopping and nodding my head back at his bedroom. I had to be careful how I handled this. He *had* stolen the stone fairy after all, and I didn't want him to try denying it just because he was too afraid of getting into trouble. "If you brought anything with you, you'll need to take it back again for this to work," I said as casually as I could.

"Brought anything with me? What do you mean?" Tommy asked, his face starting to color again — a tiny hint of pink at the top of his cheeks.

"Well, you know. If you picked anything up along the way."

"Like what?" he asked. His eyes met mine, and I knew he was challenging me. There was no other way around this. I had to tell the truth.

"Like a piece of amber," I said carefully. "We just need it to go back again so that you can get back to normal."

Tommy stared at me, his jaw wide open. "How do you know about the amber?" he asked.

"I—" I what? What could I possibly say that could make sense to him? *I'm on a mission from a place above the clouds where fairies are given assignments, and this one is part of saving the entire world from disaster?* Yeah, that would go over *really* well.

Then I remembered that I wasn't the one who had to prove myself here! "Look, we just know about it, that's all. And we need it to go back with you. So I'm just making sure you don't forget it."

Tommy looked down at the floor, shuffling his feet from side to side.

"Tommy?"

He stared at the carpet.

"Tommy, what is it?" I asked.

Eventually he looked up at me. "It's the amber," he said. "It's gone."

I stared at Tommy. He stared back. Neither of us knew what to say next.

"What do you mean, it's gone?" I asked eventually.

"I mean it's gone. I—" But before he finished whatever he was about to say, a noise downstairs made both of us jump so suddenly, we practically head-butted each other.

"What was *that*?" Tommy asked, white-faced and halfway back to his bedroom.

"That's Daisy," I said.

A moment later, a voice called up the stairs. "Philippa?"

I smiled at Tommy. "Told you," I said. "We're up here!" I called down the stairs.

"*We?*" Daisy charged up the stairs. "I knew it!" she said, coming up to join us on the landing. "I saw you come in here a while ago. I had a feeling something was going on."

Tommy was staring at Daisy, looking like a scared little boy, even though he wasn't that much younger than me. "Daisy, this is Tommy; Tommy, this is Daisy," I said, feeling only slightly ridiculous giving formal introductions at a time like this.

"Well done!" Daisy said, checking the time on her MagiCell. "Ten to eight. We're still ahead of schedule. Let's get going." She punched a few buttons as she started to walk along the landing. "I'm going to give ATC a quick update," she said.

Tommy was still staring at Daisy. He hadn't moved.

"Daisy, wait," I said. "We've got a bit of a problem." I turned to Tommy. "Do you want to tell her, or shall I?"

Tommy was pointing at Daisy. "She had one of those things, too," he said.

I looked at Daisy. "One of *what?*"

"That phone in her hand. She had one just like it."

Daisy turned around and took a couple of steps toward Tommy. "This?" she said, holding her MagiCell in front of her.

Tommy nodded.

Daisy looked at me. I looked at Tommy. Tommy looked at the floor.

"Tommy," I said. "I think you need to tell us what happened."

chapter thirteen

Tommy

They were both staring at me, waiting for me to
explain. But how could I? How could I tell them
what had happened? I'd spent my life being the butt
of everyone else's jokes, and now I'd be the same
with them — and I'd only just *met* them.

Daisy took another step closer to me. There was
something about her. I don't know what it was, but
she reminded me a bit of — of the —

"OK, I'll tell you," I said. "But on one condition."

"Go on," Daisy said.

"You don't laugh."

"Of course we won't laugh," Philippa said.

"There's nothing remotely funny about this," Daisy said in a way that made a chill sneak up my spine.

"And you have to believe me," I added. "Because everything I'm going to tell you is absolutely true."

"We believe you," Daisy said. Philippa nodded her agreement.

"OK. Well, this is what happened," I said. And then I told them everything. I told them what happened on Tuesday, when we'd done the climbing ropes as a special end-of-semester treat.

"So it was my turn to climb up the rope," I said. "And it's not my fault that I wear glasses, or that they slipped off my nose when I looked down. And it's not my fault that the laughing below made me so nervous, my hands became too sweaty to hold on to the rope."

"OK, we hear you," Daisy said.

"So then Danny picks my glasses up off the floor. 'Tiny Tommy strikes again!' he shouts, holding his arms out and waving my glasses in front of my face. I kept reaching out for them, and he kept pulling them away. Then I swung for them too hard and fell over. And that was when even the teacher started laughing."

"The teacher was laughing at you?" Philippa asked.

I nodded. "He tried to hide it — but I heard him. I wanted to curl up and die right there."

"What did you do?" Daisy asked.

"What *could* I do? I just waited for it to stop, like I always do. Eventually Mr. Petrie said something totally lame like, 'OK, that's enough now.' No punishment. Not even a scolding. Even *he* doesn't stand up to Danny Slater. No one stands up to Danny Slater."

"So what happened next?" Daisy asked.

"Apart from being tripped in the hallway and being called Wimpy Williams all day, you mean?" I said bitterly.

Daisy nodded.

"After school," Philippa said gently.

So I told them about the walk home through the woods, climbing up the rocks, finding the amber.

"And then, the moment I walked out of the circle with it, something really weird happened. It was like everything was exactly the same, but completely different, too."

Daisy nodded. "Because time had frozen," she said. She understood!

"Yes. Everything around me just stopped. Birds froze in the air, the trees didn't rustle, no wind, no nothing. And it's been like that for over a week now. At least, I think it's been that long. It's hard to tell."

"And what about the amber?" Philippa asked. "What happened to it?"

"That was the weirdest thing of all," I said. "One moment it was in my hand. The next . . ." I glanced at them both to make sure they weren't laughing. "You promise you'll believe me?"

"We promise," Daisy replied. "Honestly."

"OK. Well—the amber kind of changed. One minute, it was like a cold jagged piece of stone in my hand. The next—well, first it felt kind of fluttery, like it was tickling my hand. Then the stone disappeared completely, and all these colors burst out of it. It was like a rainbow-filled bomb had gone off in my hand!"

I glanced at them again. They were both looking seriously at me. No laughing.

"What happened next?" Daisy asked.

"The colors started making a shape. I thought it was a bird at first—but it wasn't."

"What was it?" Philippa prompted me.

"It was a —" I stopped. I couldn't do it. I couldn't say it out loud, in front of a pair of *girls*!

"Was it a fairy?" Philippa asked gently.

She knew! She knew!

I looked down at the floor and nodded.

Daisy let out a breath. "She transformed," she said. I wanted to ask what she meant, but she went on before I had the chance. "That's why she wasn't at the stone circle."

"Did she say anything?"

"No," I replied. "She just took off running."

"So she could be anywhere?" Philippa asked.

Daisy was pressing buttons on her weird-looking phone. "But it doesn't make sense," she said. "I've tried to locate her on her MagiCell but I couldn't get a reading. It should have worked if she transformed."

"Um . . ." I said.

"Maybe try again?" Philippa suggested. "The connection with Robyn wasn't great, but perhaps it'll work this time."

"Er . . ." I tried again.

"I'll try it," Daisy said. "You never know."

I cleared my throat. They both looked at me. "What?" Daisy asked impatiently.

"I don't think it's going to work," I said.

"Why not?" Philippa asked. "How would you know if it'll work or not? You don't know anything about MagiCells."

"About what?" I pointed to Daisy's phone. "You mean that?"

"That's right," Daisy said.

I reached into my pocket and felt for the thing that had fallen away from the piece of amber after it turned into a fairy. The thing she'd dropped on the ground and left behind because she was so startled when she saw me that all she seemed to want to do was run away and hide. The thing that looked exactly the same as Daisy's strange phone — apart from the broken parts and cracks across the screen. I pulled it out of my pocket.

"Erm," I said as I nervously cleared my throat again. "Is this what you're looking for?"

Daisy ✻

Tommy was holding something out toward me. I leaned in for a closer look.

"How did you get that?" I sputtered. It was a MagiCell!

"She—she dropped it," he stammered.

I took the MagiCell from him. "The fairy did?"

He nodded.

"It's not working," I said.

"I know. It fell on a rock when she dropped it. I didn't do it!"

"It's all right," Philippa said. "We're not blaming you." She turned to me. "Can you get it working again?"

I turned the MagiCell over in my hands and tinkered with the buttons. "I'll try," I said. I keyed in the restore code and waited. Ten seconds later, the screen came to life. It filled with names, numbers, lines of information. It told me the stone fairy's name, age, the color of her eyes, her previous assignments, best friend, shoe size — pretty much everything in the world I might want to know — apart from one thing. Her location.

"Oh, no," I said.

"What's the matter?" Philippa asked, looking over my shoulder at the MagiCell.

"It's not going to do much for us, I'm afraid. This is just a bank of background information on the fairy. Nothing about where she is now. She'd need to have it with her in order for us or ATC to locate her."

It was beginning to feel completely hopeless. "I don't have any other ideas and we're running out of time."

"Running out of time for what?" Tommy asked. "What do we have to do?"

I didn't have the patience to answer Tommy's questions. I know it was mean of me. Now that we knew how he'd gotten here, and we knew that he hadn't deliberately meant to steal the stone fairy, I shouldn't have been angry with him. And in a way I wasn't. I mean, he'd had a terrible time, and he didn't know what was going on—I felt sorry for him; I really did. But at the same time, I couldn't help being irritated. He might not have *intended* to do it, but it was still his fault that we were all in this mess in the first place.

"What are we going to do?" Philippa asked.

I met her eyes and wished I had an answer. I couldn't bear the thought of letting her down. She was my best friend and the one person I'd want to help out, no matter what. If she was in trouble, I'd *always* want to be there for her—and I knew she felt the same way about me.

Wait—that was it! Of course!

"Philippa—I think I know where she's gone!" I said, scrolling back through the stone fairy's information again.

"What are you looking for?" Tommy asked.

"Hold on. Nearly there . . ." I kept scrolling and then—"Got it!"

"Got *what*?" Philippa and Tommy asked in unison, each one looking over a shoulder to see what I was looking at.

"Elsie Blomley."

"Elsie who? Who on earth is that?" Philippa asked.

I turned to her and smiled. "The stone fairy's best friend!"

Philippa

"I don't get it," I said. "How does that help us?"

"It's where she'll be; I'm sure of it," Daisy said excitedly. "She's terrified, trapped, lost, alone. Where's she going to go? Who's she going to look for?"

"Of course! Her best friend!"

Daisy was looking at the stone fairy's MagiCell. "Now, all we need to do is locate Elsie Blomley's address, and I bet you a wing on the wind that's where she'll be."

But a few moments later, Daisy's shoulders sagged so heavily it was as if they'd turned to cloth. "Oh," she said.

"What is it?" Tommy asked.

Daisy turned the screen so we could see.

REQUEST INVALID flashed on the screen in bright, bouncing colors.

"It can't be invalid," Daisy said. "It's her best friend. She's in the files."

"Daisy," I said. She looked up. "I don't want to ruin your hopes or anything. I mean, I think this is a brilliant idea. But . . ."

"But what?"

"Well—how long has the stone fairy been there?"

"I'm not sure, exactly," Daisy said absently. "ATC said each one's there for a hundred years."

"That's right," I said, remembering the conversation with the fairies at High Command. "And they said she was three quarters of the way through her assignment."

"Which means she'll have been there for about seventy-five years."

"Maybe that's why your request was invalid. Her best friend is probably way dead by now!" Tommy said.

Daisy shot him a filthy look.

"What? I'm helping!"

"She might not be dead," I said to Tommy. "Maybe she just moved and can't be traced." I turned to Daisy. "What makes you think her best friend was a human, anyway?"

"All the stone fairies have to have a close relationship with a human. It's what makes them able to do their job," Daisy replied flatly.

That was when I had a thought. "Daisy, wait," I said. "Maybe we can find her."

"How?"

"Look, give me your MagiCell—the one that works."

Daisy handed me the MagiCell. "What are you going to do with it?"

I smiled at her. "I'm going to call our friend — again."

"That's right, so anything you can find about the Blomley family from about a hundred years ago," I said. "Did they move? Are they still alive? Anything at all."

"Got it," Robyn said. "I'll get back to you as soon as I've found something."

I passed the MagiCell back to Daisy and tried to prepare myself for a long and possibly fruitless wait.

Tommy cleared his throat and nudged his glasses up his nose. "Listen, I know that this is probably top secret and all that," he said. "But seeing as I'm already in the middle of it, do you think there's any chance of filling me in on what exactly is going on?"

I looked at Daisy. She hesitated. "There's no point," she said.

"What do you mean, no point?" asked Tommy.

"You won't remember."

"Why not?"

She sighed. "Look, if we ever get you out of here, you won't remember anything about it."

"What? You mean I'll have a complete blank for about a week of my life?" Tommy asked.

"Not exactly," Daisy explained. "It'll all just be a bit vague. You know how sometimes you can't quite remember what you had for dinner the night before, or what someone told you five minutes earlier? It'll be like that."

"What about my family? They'll know I've been gone!"

Daisy shook her head. "Anyone connected with your life will feel the same. Vague recollections but nothing to make them suspicious. They certainly won't remember you were missing. It'll be pretty much as though this never happened," Daisy said. "It won't even be in the newspaper anymore. It'll have vanished, along with your memories."

"What about me?" I asked. "Will it be the same for me too?"

Daisy nodded. "You've been part of the assignment in real time, so you'll remember everything — Robyn will, too."

"Wow," Tommy said. "Well, if I won't remember, and we can't do anything till we hear back from your friend, you might as well tell me."

Daisy pursed her lips as she considered it. "OK," she said eventually, "but we can't tell you everything."

"Just tell me what you can."

So we did. Between us, we explained about the stone fairies and the portals and the friendships from the old days. We explained a bit about ATC and all the different assignments. The only department we didn't tell him about was EDD, and their predictions for the future. That was the bit we knew we couldn't tell *anyone* — whether they would remember it afterward or not. It was too terrible to think about.

We'd pretty much covered everything when Daisy's MagiCell buzzed.

"Robyn!" I grabbed the MagiCell and put it on speakerphone. "Have you got anything for us?" I asked before she'd even said hello.

"Well, I've got *something* — but I'm not sure how much help it'll be."

"It'll be better than anything *we've* got," Daisy said.

"Right. Well, first I tried the local phone book to see if there's a Blomley family living locally. That was obviously too much to hope for. There's nothing. So then I looked up the name online. Couldn't find anything around here at first. But then I dug a bit deeper, and I found something."

"What?" I asked.

"Well, there *was* a Blomley family nearby. Robert and Vera Blomley. And guess what?"

"They had a daughter?" Tommy suggested.

"Who was *that*?" Robyn asked. I suddenly remembered we hadn't told her where we were, or mentioned anything about Tommy. And we still couldn't. *Tommy* might not have any recollection of any of this once we got him out of here — if we ever did! But since Robyn would remember everything, and until we knew there wasn't going to be anything to panic about, we couldn't take the risk.

"He's helping us," Daisy said quickly. "Go on."

"OK," Robyn said. She sounded annoyed, and I wished we could tell her everything.

"Anyway, yes," she went on. "They had a daughter — Elsie!"

"Bingo!" I shouted.

"So, have you got an address?" Daisy asked.

"Well, that's the tricky part. They worked at Henley House, on the edge of the village. Robert was the butler and Vera worked in the kitchens."

"Henley House?" I asked. I was pretty sure I'd read about a place called Henley House in a brochure. "But that still exists, doesn't it?"

"The house itself does. It's open to the public now — we've got brochures about it in the shop."

"So what's the problem?" Daisy asked.

"Well, there are two problems. The first is that Elsie either got married or changed her name, or left the area — or worse — because I haven't managed to find any trace of her."

"And the other?" I asked, wondering what could be more of a problem than the fact that the person we were looking for had disappeared without a trace.

"Well, they lived in one of the servants' houses on the estate," Robyn said. "All of which have been knocked down."

"Knocked down?" Daisy burst out. "Why?"

Robyn hesitated for a second, then said, almost apologetically, "To build a theme park."

*   *   *

"What are we going to do?" I asked. I didn't really expect an answer. There wasn't one. The only lead we had had disappeared without a trace. Even her *house* had been knocked down!

Daisy was sitting on the floor with her head in her hands. "I don't know," she said. "But we're going to have to think quickly. We're running out of time." She checked her MagiCell. "It's past nine o'clock! We've got less than three hours to sort this out, or else . . ."

She didn't need to finish her sentence. I knew how disastrous the second half of it was — and I'm pretty sure Tommy did too, even if he didn't know the details.

Wait! That was it! You didn't always have to know the whole truth of something to *think* you knew it. The stone fairy wouldn't know the whole truth about her friend, either.

"Daisy — we should go there anyway!" I said.

"Go where?"

"The theme park. The place where Elsie used to live."

"What's the point?" Daisy asked. "She's not there, her family's not there, her house isn't there."

"It doesn't matter!" I cried.

"What do you mean it doesn't matter? How can it not—"

"Because your fairy doesn't know that," Tommy said.

I looked at him. "Exactly."

Daisy stared at us both for a moment. A second later, she was on her feet. "Of course!" she said. "Come on—let's go. There's no time to waste."

Henley House was about a mile from Tommy's house. We ran nearly all the way. Luckily Tommy knew a shortcut through the woods—although I have to say, running through a forest in virtual darkness with everything around me frozen and silent is perhaps the creepiest thing I've ever done in my life.

We got to the other side of the woods and looked around. "Now where?" I asked, resting against a fence as I got my breath back.

"Um." Tommy looked frantically around. "I'm not sure."

"What do you mean you're not sure?" Daisy snapped. "Think! We're running out of time."

"Look, I'm doing the best I can," Tommy snapped back. "If I wasn't here, you wouldn't even have known what direction Henley House was in."

"If you weren't here, none of us would be in this mess in the first place!" Daisy snarled.

Tommy didn't say anything else after that.

We trudged across fields, looking all around us as we walked. After a while, a big building came into view in the distance. It looked very grand, with turrets at each end, a dome in the middle, and a row of newish-looking outbuildings to each side. "What's that?" I asked, pointing at it.

Tommy pushed his glasses up his nose and looked

across to where I was pointing. "That's it!" he said. "That's Henley House — come on!"

And with that, he charged off and led the way across the fields. Daisy and I followed behind, and all I could do was hope that we really were heading for the right place.

chapter fourteen

Daisy

My nerves were beginning to rattle. We'd scoured the whole theme park and hadn't found anything yet.

We'd run the length of a mini train track full of people midwave with frozen grins slapped across their faces. We'd scanned the silent halls of a stately home, surrounded by people standing in front of paintings, as solid and still as the suits of armor beside them. We'd explored every bit of the zoo, examining the cages of monkeys staring out through the bars of their cages, suspended on one arm from a tree. One of them must have been midleap from branch to branch—he was actually frozen in midair! We'd been everywhere. No stone fairy. Nothing.

I was beginning to think we'd gotten it completely wrong. Amber simply wasn't here. It was obvious. I checked my MagiCell. Twenty past ten! This was awful! We were going to fail. We really were going to be trapped here forever! My breath caught in my throat, almost choking me.

"Hey!" Tommy was running toward me. "Daisy, I think I've found something. Come on, quick."

We ran along a lane and around the corner, then down a narrow path I hadn't noticed before, and out the other side.

"More theme park rides," I said, looking around. Where would we even start? We couldn't afford any more dead ends. We simply didn't have time.

"Not just any rides," Tommy said. "Look. Hurry!" He pulled me over to an entrance with a placard outside it.

"'Hedge Maze,'" I read from the placard. "'The biggest and best in the world!'"

"Look!" He was pointing at the picture in the center of the maze, with a title above it.

"'The Fairy Garden,'" I read.

"Exactly. That's where she'll be! I'll bet you anything!"

I stared at the picture, and the words, and then at Tommy.

He looked back at me, his confidence slipping a little. "It's got to at least be worth a try, right?" he asked.

For a moment, I wanted to cry with despair. He'd brought me to a toy fairy garden! But then I thought again. Maybe he was right. If the stone fairy saw this picture, she wouldn't necessarily know it was only a tourist attraction. She *might* think it would feel like home.

"You know what, Tommy?" I said. "It just might be."

Tommy ran over to grab Philippa, and we made our way into the maze.

"This way," Tommy said, turning left at the first T junction.

"How do you know?" Philippa asked.

Tommy shrugged. "Just a guess."

"Well, I think it's *this* way." Philippa turned right.

Tommy shrugged again. "Fine." We turned right and hit a dead end almost immediately.

"Um . . ." Tommy said.

"OK, you were right, come on," Philippa said sharply, and we turned left again.

But as we followed path after path, took wrong turn after wrong turn, and hit dead end after dead end, everyone's tempers started to fray.

"Daisy, why can't you just fly there?" Philippa asked after we came to a dead end we'd already reached three times.

"I can't. Not here. It's one of the things about this place. I don't have those powers."

"What powers *do* you have?" Tommy asked.

"Here, not a lot. Mainly just my MagiCell."

"Why not use that, then?" Tommy asked. "Can't it find our way around?"

"How's it supposed to do that?" I snapped.

"Look." Philippa pointed to a sign in front of us. LIFT FOR CLUE, it said. We lifted it.

"Exit that way," Philippa read aloud. There was a hand pointing left.

"But we don't want the exit," I complained.

"Wait—maybe we do," Tommy said. "Where we came in, they had postcards with a picture of the maze on them."

"So if we go out and come back in again, we could use a postcard to help us find our way around?" Philippa asked.

Tommy smiled. "Exactly."

"Come on, then," I said. "No time to lose."

We tore through the maze, following clues all the way to the exit. Eventually we were out. Tommy ran over to the ticket office and grabbed a postcard. We huddled around it, examining the route.

"Wow—it looks pretty easy," Tommy said.

I shot him a look. "Anything's easy when you've got the solution in your hand," I said. "Come on, let's go."

Philippa

"OK, left at the next junction, then around this bend, and then—" I looked up from the postcard. "That's it!"

We'd done it! We'd found the fairy garden in the middle of the maze.

"Wow," Tommy said, turning around to survey the fairy garden. "*Look* at it!"

A perfect green lawn with trees dotted all over it, a row of tiny stone cottages, with some steps made from logs leading up a hill—all in miniature! A river ran through the middle of it all, with a stone bridge across it. Here and there, little doors formed entrances into the hill. And hidden in nooks and crannies all over the place were little fairies!

One of them was sitting on a swing looped over a tree's branch. Another sat at the water's edge just below the bridge. The more I looked, the more of them I saw. They were absolutely everywhere!

"We haven't got time to look around," Daisy said. "We need to find Amber."

A second later, Tommy gasped and clapped a hand over his mouth. He pulled at my sleeve. "Philippa,

come with me," he whispered out of the corner of his mouth. Then he whispered out of the other corner, "Daisy, come on. Don't say anything, and don't make it obvious."

He walked a few steps away from the fairy garden, in an exaggerated impression of someone trying to look casual. Daisy and I followed, giving each other any-idea-what-this-is-about looks.

Tommy leaned in toward us. "She's here," he whispered.

"What?" Daisy nearly shouted. "How do you know?"

"Shh, don't give it away!" he stage-whispered back at her.

"Which one is she?" I asked, turning around to look again.

"Don't make it obvious!" Tommy hissed. "She clearly doesn't want us to find her, or she wouldn't be trying to disguise herself as one of these. She's halfway up the hill behind the bridge."

I pretended to scratch my neck and turned around so I could see where he meant. "The one with long hair?"

"Yes. The only one who looks as though she's paused in the middle of trying to get somewhere."

Now that he mentioned it, I could see what he meant. She did look as though she was midpace, and all the others seemed to be either sitting or leaning against something.

Daisy looked across too. "That's not really enough to prove she's —"

"And the fact that she's a bit bigger than the others," Tommy went on.

Daisy snorted. "Hardly! And that's not exactly —"

"And the fact that I've already seen her, remember! When she flew out of my hand?"

I stared at Tommy, mouth open. Daisy did one quick double take from Tommy to the fairy and back again. "You're absolutely sure?" she asked.

"Positive," Tommy said seriously.

"Right," she said. And with that, she stomped right up to the fairy before I'd even had a chance to close my mouth.

Daisy grabbed the fairy and lifted it up. "It's you, isn't it?" she said.

The fairy didn't reply. It didn't move.

Daisy shook the fairy. "Tell me!" she shouted at it, holding it tightly in her hand. "You're the stone fairy, aren't you? Not *a* stone fairy like these ones — you're *the* stone fairy. *Aren't* you?"

The fairy still didn't move. I was beginning to think Tommy had gotten it all wrong. "Daisy, are you sure —"

"Answer me!" Daisy squeezed the fairy harder — and then, all of a sudden, the fairy made a sound. She let out a breath! It *was* her!

The fairy gasped for breath. "You're hurting me!" she said. "You're holding me too tight!"

"I'm not letting go till you admit it," Daisy said. "Answer my question. Are you Amber?"

The fairy stared up at Daisy for a silent few moments. Then, finally, she lowered her eyes. "Yes," she said in a voice so quiet, we might have missed it if it wasn't so still and silent all around us. "I'm the one you're looking for. I'm the stone fairy."

"What were you doing?" Daisy shouted at the fairy. "Why were you hiding like that?"

The fairy lowered her head. "I'm sorry," she said. "Look, please just let me down, and I'll tell you."

"No chance."

"*Please.* I promise I won't run away."

"Daisy, put her on the ground," I said. "She can't get very far with all three of us watching her every move."

Daisy opened her hand. "If you even *try* —"

"I won't," she said firmly.

Daisy glared at her for a moment, then set her back down on the ground.

The fairy shook herself, then looked around at all three of us. "So you know who I am?" she asked.

"You're Amber," I replied.

"The stone fairy," Tommy added.

She nodded. "And I'm guessing you've come to take me back to the stone circle, so I can get back to my job."

"That's right," Daisy said, glancing at her Magi-Cell. "And we need to get a move on. We've got just over an hour to get back!"

"Right," Amber said. "Well, in that case, I'd better tell you something important."

"Amber, tell us quickly," I begged. I was getting so impatient, my teeth were starting to itch!

"Very well." She pressed her lips together and rubbed her chin. Then she nodded, as though making an agreement with herself. "Here's the thing," she said. "I'm not going back."

"You're not going back?" Daisy yelled in a high-pitched screech. "What do you mean, you're not going back? You most definitely are going back, if I have to drag you there my —"

"Daisy, wait." I put a hand on her arm. I'd never seen her like this. Even when we first met and I accidentally threw her out of the window, she wasn't as angry as this. "Let Amber tell us the full story."

"The full story?" Daisy snapped. "We haven't got *time* to hear her story!"

"I'd say we haven't got time *not* to hear it," Tommy said. "It doesn't look like she's going to do what you say if we don't."

"You should listen to your friends," Amber said to Daisy. "They're talking sense. You could drag me back to the stone circle, but you cannot return me to my work without my agreement."

Daisy's face was scarlet. "Go on, then," she said between tight lips. "But talk quickly."

Amber nodded. "In the fairy godmother world, we are used to making sacrifices. It is part of the job, and we all accept that. But in truth, nobody really understands the sacrifice that a stone fairy makes. Way beyond any other."

Daisy rolled her eyes.

"You might doubt it," Amber said, turning on her. "But *you* try giving up every single power you have, even the ability to *move*! Then stay like that for a hundred years!"

Daisy and Amber stared at each other like two dogs trying to decide whether to fight or run. Eventually, Amber broke her gaze. "I wouldn't have minded," she went on. "I accepted the responsibility and I took the vow. But do you know why?" She looked at us all.

I shook my head. "Why?"

Amber turned to me. "Because in my heart of hearts, I didn't really believe it would be as hard as they said."

"As who said?" Tommy asked.

"ATC." Amber looked at Daisy. "I was like you," she said. "Fiery and righteous. Always knew I was right." She nudged her head toward me. "And with a best friend like yours, too."

"A human, you mean?" I asked.

Amber looked taken aback. "I didn't know you were human! Well, yes, in that case, that as well! But I meant the loyalty." She paused. "Imagine for a moment that you two made each other a promise. Would you keep it?"

"Of course!" Daisy and I said in unison.

"Exactly. You'd honor it, no matter what. And if someone told you that you had to do something that meant you'd never be able to see each other again, would you do whatever you could to stop that from happening?"

Daisy nodded. "Yes, I would," she said.

"Anything," I added.

Amber folded her arms as though she'd won the whole argument.

"But I don't understand," I said. "What are you saying?"

"Is this about Elsie?" Tommy asked.

For a second, Amber looked trapped. "You know about Elsie?"

"How else do you think we tracked you down here?" Daisy asked.

"Elsie was my best friend," Amber said sadly. "We met when I was on an assignment for ATC."

"Exactly like us!" I burst out.

"I was working for IRD."

"Illness and Recovery Department?" Daisy asked.

Amber nodded. "Elise had food poisoning and I helped her get over it. We hit it off immediately."

Daisy looked at me and made a face. "*Not* exactly like us then!"

Amber went on. "When I took this job, they told me I would have to say good-bye to her, that I'd never see her again. But I didn't really believe it. I *refused* to believe it. In fact, I was so determined to find a way that I made her a promise."

"What did you promise?" Tommy asked.

"That I *would* see her again. I don't know how I thought I could do it. I don't know what made me believe that my determination was greater than my responsibility to ATC. I just knew that Elsie was my best friend, and I *was* going to see her again."

"But that was—what? Seventy years ago?" Tommy said.

"Seventy-two," Amber replied.

I cleared my throat. How did I put this? "Amber, maybe she's, um, I mean have you thought about the possibility that she might be . . ."

"Yes. She might be dead by now. I know that," Amber said. "But something in my heart tells me she's alive. She'll be eighty-four! All these years, I've imagined the look on her face when I turn up and shout, 'Surprise!' Even *I* had begun to doubt that this day would ever come. It's hard to keep your belief for three quarters of a century, you know." Amber looked at Tommy and smiled. "But thanks to you, I have a chance—my one and only chance. I want to find her. I *have* to find her," she said. "And I'm not going back until I do."

Daisy looked again at her MagiCell. For the first time since we'd found Amber, she spoke almost softly. "Look, I understand. I really do," she said. "But you can't! We've got less than an hour now. We *have* to get back. You don't understand. If we don't get back by midnight . . ."

Daisy stopped and glared at Tommy.

"Daisy, just tell her!" I said. "It doesn't matter anymore. In an hour's time, we're *all* doomed! Tell her!"

"Look, it doesn't make any difference, whatever you want to tell me," Amber said. "I've made up my mind—and there's nothing you can say that will change it. I can't go back to that stone. I have to find Elsie!"

"But she'll be frozen in time, like everyone else here!" Tommy burst out, looking as panic-stricken as me and Daisy, possibly because of hearing the words *we're all doomed*.

Amber shook her head. "I don't care. I need to see her—one way or another—before it's too late. I promised!" She nodded at me and Daisy. "It's just like you two. She's my best friend."

Daisy stared at Amber. "You don't realize what you're doing. We've got more information than they had in your day. The fairy and human worlds will be severed forever—you're condemning the world to utter disaster!"

"You're exaggerating," Amber said. "ATC will find a way around all of it, I'm sure. It'll be OK. It won't be as bad as you think."

"As bad as we think?" I shouted. "You haven't

seen the images of the future! *I* have! It's *not* going
to be OK! You're kidding yourself, just like you did
with your stupid promise! It's NOT going to be
OK. You have to come with us!"

Amber shook her head again. "I'm sorry," she said.
"I really am. But I've decided. I'm not going until I
can see Elsie."

I turned to Daisy. "Daisy—do something!" I
screamed. I couldn't bear it. To have come this far.
To have found the stone fairy with only an hour
to spare, and now this. We were going to be stuck
here forever. I'd never see Robyn again, or Mom
and Dad—or anyone!

Daisy was pressing buttons on her MagiCell.
She didn't reply. I grabbed her arm. "Please!"

Daisy shrugged my hand off and put her Magi-
Cell to her ear. "Just give me a minute," she said.
And then she walked away.

That was it, then. Even Daisy had given up! The
moment she turned her back and walked away was
the moment I knew it was over.

I sat down on the ground and started saying my
prayers.

chapter fifteen

Daisy

I hunched over my MagiCell, talking as quietly as I could.

"So what do you say?" I asked.

Chara paused for a long time. "You are absolutely sure about this, FG32561?"

"I'm positive," I replied. "There's no other way."

"You understand the sacrifice you are making? You are clear about all the implications of this decision?"

"I am," I replied. "She hasn't seen what EDD predicted. She doesn't understand, and I haven't got time to convince her. But I *have* seen it, and I know there's no other choice."

"You are a generous soul, you know," Chara said.

"Thank you," I replied, glad she couldn't see me blush at her praise, and relieved she didn't know the true mix of emotions that was swirling inside me with this decision.

"Very well, then," she said. "We will allow it."

I let out a huge breath. "Thank you," I said. "Thank you."

"Go now," Chara replied. "You have no time to waste."

I switched off my MagiCell and ran back to the others. "OK," I said. "I've figured it out. We need to go."

"I've already told you, I'm not going," Amber said. "I'm going to look for my friend."

"You *can* look for her," I snapped. Just because I'd made a huge sacrifice didn't mean I was *happy* about it—or happy that she'd put me into a position where it was my only option. It wasn't so much myself I was worried about. Yes, the whole world was hanging on our actions here—but most importantly, I couldn't bear to think of Philippa being trapped here forever, never seeing her parents or Robyn or anyone she cared about ever again. I wasn't going to do that to her.

"I've made a deal with ATC," I went on. "If you go back to your job as the stone fairy, you'll be allowed to travel between the human and fairy worlds and move around whenever you want, provided you are at the portal whenever you're needed. So you *can* look for your friend—in her world. Plus the rest of us can get back there, too."

"But how—how did you do that?" Philippa asked.

"It doesn't matter," I said. I couldn't look her in the eye. "All that matters is that we get back, quickly."

"This isn't a trick, is it?" Amber asked. "You've really made that deal?"

"I've really made the deal," I said.

"You promise?" Amber asked. She looked at me with such gratitude and such hope that all of a sudden, I realized she was the same as me. She *did* care about the world, and about all of us.

She just cared about her best friend most of all.

I met her eyes and smiled. "I promise."

Philippa

We ran back to the portal so fast, my heart felt as though it had fire coursing through it. We reached the stone circle with fifteen minutes to spare. All we had to do now was link hands and recite the poem for taking us back through the hole in time—and *pray* that it would work.

I'd tried asking Daisy about the deal she'd made with ATC but she wouldn't tell me. She wouldn't even look at me—in fact she'd hardly spoken all the way here. *What had she done?*

"Are you ready?" Daisy asked, looking around at us all.

Only Tommy hesitated.

"What's wrong?" I asked.

He shrugged. "I don't know. I mean — I'm glad to be going back. *Really* glad — of course I am."

"What, then?"

"Just — there are some things I'd rather not be going back to. Or rather — some people."

"The bully? Danny?"

Tommy nodded. "I mean, I know that living in this frozen place has been like being trapped inside a nightmare — but at least I didn't have to put up with *him*." He laughed. "D'you know what I did one day?"

Daisy glanced at her MagiCell, probably checking we had enough time for Tommy's story. "We've got time," I said sternly. Then I turned back to Tommy. "What did you do?"

"I went to his house. He was sitting in front of his TV, feet up on a chair with his boots on, half a bag of chips in his mouth, frozen solid like everyone else. I went up to him with a marker and drew spots all over his face, and a big, thick pair of glasses to match. Every time I needed cheering up, I went over to look at him!" Tommy paused. "He didn't look half as scary like that," he went on. "But now I'm going back to the real world, and he'll be back to the real Danny Slater again, won't he? Calling me a wimp in front of everyone, making me a laughing-stock at every opportunity."

"But you're not a *wimp!*" I said. "You're about to help save the whole world from disaster!"

"Yeah, but he'll never know that, will he? I'm not exactly going to go around telling people I went into another realm where time froze, met up with a couple of fairies, and happened to save the planet. I'd be bullied from here to eternity for coming up with a story like that!"

Daisy pressed some buttons on her MagiCell. "Right," she said.

Tommy turned to her. "I mean, you told me that it'll be as though I'd never been gone. So it's back to the same old thing—constant taunting. It doesn't exactly fill me with joy, that's all."

"I wouldn't be so sure things will be *exactly* the same," Daisy said, smiling as she put her MagiCell away. "You never know what ATC can come up with when you ask nicely."

"What do you mean?" Tommy asked.

Daisy tapped her nose. "You'll see," she replied. "Let's just say, time sometimes leaves its mark."

And with that she headed for the center of the circle and called us all over. "This is it. We've got ten minutes. Everyone ready?"

Tommy and Amber nodded.

Daisy turned to me. "You know what's going to happen now?"

"We go back to the normal world?"

Daisy nodded. "As soon as we go through the hole in time, we each come out in our own place. You and Tommy on Earth, I'll be back at ATC, and Amber will be back in place here."

I nodded. "Got it."

Daisy swallowed. "So we should say good-bye," she said quietly.

I laughed. "Well, yes. For now — but I'll see you soon."

Daisy swallowed again. Her eyes were shiny. And then I noticed something else — a tear rolling down her cheek.

"Daisy?"

She shook her head. Then she threw her arms around me and hugged me so tightly I couldn't breathe. "Just take really good care of yourself," she said hoarsely.

"Of course I will!" I replied. "But why the tears? You're acting like we're never going to see each other again!" I laughed. "Daisy?"

She wouldn't meet my eyes. I turned cold as stone inside.

"Daisy — we *are* going to see each other again, aren't we?"

She didn't look up.

"Daisy, tell me!"

"It was all I could think of!" she cried, tears streaking down both of her cheeks now. "I didn't have any choice. I asked ATC if there was any way she'd be able to do her job but still travel around. At first they said no. In order to let the portal create a bridge to allow fairies to travel between the human and fairy worlds, it needs a fairy to give up her power to do the same. But I pushed them. I said there *had* to be another way; it was our only hope. And eventually they said perhaps there could be. They weren't sure it would work, but they agreed it was the only possibility."

I suddenly realized what Daisy had done. "The stone fairy can fulfill her assignment, but the portal will take its power from you, instead of from her so she can look for her friend."

Daisy nodded.

"So once we're back, and you get to ATC, that's it — you'll have lost your power to travel between the worlds?"

"That's right."

I stared at Daisy, trying to believe her but not wanting to. "So this really is good-bye?"

Daisy nodded. I swallowed hard. I wouldn't let myself cry. If Daisy could make a sacrifice as big as this, I would do everything I could to support her. I wasn't going to make it harder.

Amber spoke for the first time since we'd arrived at the stone circle. "You're a very special fairy," she said. "I don't believe there are many who would have made that decision."

Daisy tried to smile. She didn't get very far. I gave her the biggest hug I could without squeezing the life out of her. "It'll be OK," I said, hoping she believed me more than I did.

Daisy held her hands out, reaching down so that Amber could take one. Tommy took the other. Then they both held my hands, so we formed a circle of our own, with the rest of the stones forming a larger one around us.

Daisy met my eyes. "Ready?" she asked.

I smiled at her, hoping that with just a smile I could convey all that I wanted. That my smile could say good-bye and good luck, and thank you and I'll miss you and I'll never forget you, all at the same time.

She smiled back, and I could tell she understood—and that she was saying the same things to me.

Then Amber spoke. "Daisy, I can never thank you enough for what you've done," she said, "but I hope you know I will always, *always* be grateful."

Daisy smiled at Amber. "I know," she said softly. Then she looked at the rest of us. "OK, let's do it," she said.

And then together we recited the poem from ATC. Tommy and Amber had memorized it on the way up.

> *Circle in and circle out,*
> *Take us home tonight.*
> *Put us back where we belong,*
> *And make all wrong things right.*

I held tightly on to Amber's and Tommy's hands and held Daisy's eyes all the way. We spun together, through the darkness, through the circle of rainbow colors, and finally through a white light that was so blinding I had to let go and shield my eyes.

I opened my eyes. I was in the middle of the stone circle — in the pitch darkness of the night.

I rubbed my eyes and looked around. Beyond the stones, crowds of people were gathered, eating hot chestnuts and warming their hands in front of a roaring fire that lit the dark night, everyone smiling and laughing. Nearby, church bells were chiming. The people were counting down with the chimes.

"Three!" the crowd roared. "Two! One — Happy New Year!"

A blaze of fireworks shot noisily into the sky. I watched them and began to laugh. We'd *done* it! We'd really, truly done it!

I turned around to find Daisy. And then I remembered.

I looked at the fireworks soaring up into the sky and wondered if she was looking at them too, from her side of all this, if she could see me, if she had a great big hole inside her the same shape as the one inside me.

I glanced up to the stone in the middle of the circle, hoping that Amber had gotten back safely, and reminding myself that she must have, or else none of this would have worked.

That was when I noticed Tommy. He was sitting on top of the stone, a group of kids standing on the ground around him.

I wandered over to see what was going on.

"I don't really know how I got up here," he was saying to them. "I guess I just climbed."

"That's so amazing," one of the girls said, looking up at him with big, admiring eyes. "You're so cool!"

Tommy smiled shyly at the girl. Then one of the boys held a hand up to him. "Come on, man, I'll give you a hand down if you like. You'll be in massive trouble if they catch you up there."

"Thanks," Tommy said awkwardly. I smiled to myself as I watched.

Just then, he glanced over toward me. For a moment, he looked as if he was going to wave. Then he screwed his eyes up as though he was trying to figure out who I was.

"Do I know you?" he asked. "You look familiar."

I smiled back. It had worked just like Daisy had said it would. He didn't remember a thing — just a vague, hazy sense of something. I didn't think he'd believe me if I told him the truth, so I didn't bother trying. "I think I've seen you around," I said.

I turned to go and almost bumped into a boy running over toward Tommy and his new friends. "Look over there!" he said. Another group of kids the same age was gathered around in a huddle. They all had hands over their mouths and were bent double laughing hysterically and pointing at someone. I followed the line of their hands to see who they were pointing at.

There was a stocky boy kicking up dirt and waving his arms in the air. "What?" he snarled. "Don't you *dare* laugh at me! What's so funny?"

No one answered him. They were too busy laughing. He certainly wasn't scaring anyone with his threats. I looked at his face, and all at once I got the joke. His face was covered in spots, with a huge, thick pair of horn-rimmed glasses painted around his eyes. And he didn't even know it.

Let's just say that time sometimes leaves its mark.

I looked up at the sky and smiled. "Nice one, Daisy," I said out loud, and then I walked away and left Tommy to join his friends, laughing at the loser who used to be a bully.

As I watched the colors bursting into life in the sky, I wished so much that Daisy could have been sharing this. That we could have just a bit more time together.

But I knew that at some point I would have to accept the truth. There wasn't going to be any more time together — ever.

The thought hurt so much, it was as though one of the fireworks was shooting through me.

"Philippa!" Someone was calling me. I looked up.

"Robyn!" I yelled. Of course—I was supposed to be here with her tonight. We were meeting up with my parents together! We ran over to each other and jumped up and down in a huge, happy hug.

"You're back!" Robyn cried. "You are back, aren't you? Back for good?"

"Yes," I said. "I'm back for good."

"Hey, what are you two kids so happy about?"

I spun around. Dad! I threw my arms around him. Mom was behind him. I grabbed her too and hugged both of them as hard as I could. I never wanted to let them go.

"Hey, hey, hey," Dad said, prising my arms from around his neck and holding me out to look at me. "This is a nice welcome. And we missed you too, chicken—even if you have only been out for the day!"

"Silly old fool," Mom said, smiling as she nudged him in the ribs. "I mean, it's not as if you've been to the other side of the world and back!"

I looked at Robyn and then back at my parents—and burst out laughing. Robyn looked at me. Soon, she started laughing as well.

"What's so funny?" Mom asked, but then she started giggling too. A minute later, all four of us were laughing so hard, we all had tears rolling down our cheeks. None of the others really knew what the joke was — and none of them knew that only half of my tears were from laughing.

Robyn's dad and Annie came to join us and we all stood warming ourselves by the fire, huddled in a group, sharing a bag of hot chestnuts and looking up at the sky.

Dad squeezed in between me and Robyn and slung an arm around us both. "So, what sort of no good have you girls been up to today, then?" he asked.

How was I going to answer that? "Oh, you know, just hanging out," I said eventually.

Just then a firework whizzed up into the blackness and exploded into a giant bouquet that reached across the sky.

"Wow, look at that!" my dad said.

"I tell you what — I think this is the most spectacular New Year's Eve ever," Mom said, coming up behind me. "It's different from anything we've ever had before, isn't it?"

I smiled at Mom and wondered if she would ever say anything so true again. "Yes, Mom," I replied. "It certainly is."

chapter sixteen

Daisy

I sat at my desk, staring into space. Any minute now, they'd be here to take me to High Command. They were going to hold a big ceremony for me, tell the whole of ATC how I'd saved us all from disaster. I'd be praised by everyone for my sacrifice. I couldn't travel between the two worlds anymore, but I'd probably get a huge promotion at ATC. If not a promotion, then some kind of reward. I'd be a heroine.

So why wasn't I happy?

Why was I scratching around in my brain for something that *mattered* to me about all of that?

Why did I feel as though I'd had a hole dug out of the middle of me?

I knew the answer. Because none of it meant as much to me as the thought that I was never going to see Philippa again. *Ever.*

I picked things up off my desk and put them down again, trying to make some sort of order, tidy up a bit, get back to normal.

Normal—what was that, anyway? One assignment after another? A world that didn't mean anything to me anymore?

I pulled my drawer open and angrily shoved some paper work inside it.

And that was when I saw it.

I checked around to make sure no one was watching me, and then I reached inside my drawer. I stared at it for ages. The box that Philippa had been given, with the one-trip-only portal code inside: the code that anyone could use, even if they didn't have the power to move between the two worlds.

I could use it now! I could see Philippa again!

I pressed a finger to my mouth and bit into my nail. Could I? It was a one-way trip. If I did it, I'd be leaving ATC forever. And probably giving up all the rest of my fairy powers too.

Could I?

I had to think quickly because any minute now they'd be here to pick me up—and once everyone heard about what I'd done, I'd probably never get another moment to myself. They might even remember and take the voucher away, now that the job was done. Then I'd *definitely* be stuck here for good.

I looked around at the office. Being part of ATC meant being part of something incredibly magical.

But then I remembered the night I'd had at Philippa's house when her parents thought I was her, when I'd felt for a moment what it was like to be part of a real family. That was magical, too.

Friendship was magical.

Should I?

The wall at the far end of the office was turning into a door. This was it. They were coming. They'd be in the office any second now. I glanced behind me. If I ran, I could get out the back way before they reached my desk.

Think! Decide!

I gripped the box in my hands. What should I do? *What should I do?*

And then they came through the door. They looked around the office. Two more seconds and they'd see me. I imagined the ceremony they would hold for me. The congratulations, the praise, the promotion, all of it—and I felt sick and trapped.

It wasn't what I wanted.

I knew what I had to do. I shoved the box in my pocket, ducked low—and ran as fast as I could to the exit at the back of the office.

Philippa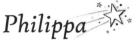

The fireworks were over. People had started drifting away. Our little group still stood staring into the glowing remains of the bonfire, watching orange slithers chase each other up and down the sticks and twigs on the ground.

I wished Daisy were here to share it with us.

"Looks like the party's over," Dad said. "Shall we head home?"

We started to walk away, the adults up ahead, Robyn and me following behind. It was the first time we'd had a chance to talk.

"So when are you going to tell me what this was all about?" Robyn asked. "Or are you still not allowed?"

I thought about Daisy up at ATC, us down here, never meeting up again. What harm could it do?

"I think I can probably tell you now," I said.

I was about to begin when Robyn looked over my shoulder, back toward the stone circle. "Or I guess Daisy could tell me, if you prefer?" she said.

I stopped walking. "Robyn, there's something I need to tell you about Daisy," I said.

Robyn laughed. "Er, there's something I need to tell *you* about Daisy!" she said.

"What?"

Robyn pointed behind me, a wide grin on her face. "She's right behind you!"

I spun around. She was right! Daisy was here! I stared at her for a moment. Then I grabbed her arm and squeezed it.

"Ouch!" Daisy said.

"You're real!"

"Of course she's real!" Robyn said.

I grabbed Daisy and hugged her tight, spinning around in a circle and laughing.

"You're acting as though you thought you were never going to see her again!" Robyn said.

"I *did* think that!" I said. "How did you — how come — are you —"

Daisy laughed. "I'm here to stay," she said. "If that's OK with you."

I threw my head back and laughed. "That's very, very, *very* OK with me!"

Just then Mom turned around to see what the commotion was. "Oh, I didn't realize you had another friend here." She waited for us to catch up.

"Mom, this is Daisy," I said.

Mom squinted at her. "Wait a minute, I think I recognize you. Aren't you from Philippa's school? We met once, didn't we?"

"That's right," Daisy said. "I'm — um —"

"Daisy's here with her parents," I said quickly. "But they said she can stay with us tonight if it's OK with you. And maybe tomorrow night, too?"

Mom smiled. "I didn't realize you were such good friends."

Daisy, Robyn, and I just looked at one another and burst out laughing.

"Can she?" I asked again. "*Please.*"

"You're sure it's all right with your parents, Daisy?"

"Positive. Honestly," Daisy replied with a big innocent smile.

Mom sighed. "Go on, then, as long as you're sure."

I threw my arms around her. "Thanks, Mom," I said. "You're the best."

My dad and Robyn's dad had stopped to wait for us. "Hey, look at that," Dad said, pointing at the ground just behind us. In the darkness, I could see the bright orange eyes of a kitten. It seemed to have come out of nowhere.

"Ohh, it's so sweet! A little tabby kitten," Robyn cried, bending down to stroke it, but it slunk away from her and rubbed itself against Daisy's leg.

Daisy bent down to stroke the kitten. Purring, it leaped up and huddled instantly into a ball in her arms.

"Well, it likes you!" Dad said. "I think you might have to keep it."

"Can it come back with Daisy tonight?" I asked.

"Good grief—anything else you want?" Dad said with a wink. Then he looked again at the kitten in Daisy's arms and laughed. "If we can't find its owner then I suppose we'll have to," he said. "We can't leave a tiny thing like that out here on its own."

Daisy smiled. "Thanks, Mr. Fisher," she said. "I'll be really careful with it."

Dad turned back and continued walking. "Come on, guys," he called back to us. "Let's go home."

I looked at Daisy. She was smiling a broad, happy smile. I had never seen her smile like that before.

"What?" I asked.

"Home," she said. "That sounds nice."

We walked back across the woods, and into the village, back to our cottage. We begged Mom and Dad to let Robyn stay over too, and we made up extra beds for them both.

The three of us sat up talking until it was light, with Daisy's new kitten curled up in her lap the whole time. We talked about everything that had happened and tried to figure out what was going to happen next.

We'd have to think of a story for Daisy, and find her somewhere to stay. Maybe she'd be able to move in with Annie — at least Annie already knew who Daisy was, so we wouldn't have to pretend. Or maybe one day we'd even tell my parents everything, and she could live with us. If there were any parents in the world likely to believe who Daisy really was, surely it was mine!

"I just can't help wondering how it'll all work out," I said.

"Me too," Robyn agreed. "But hey, at least we've got each other."

"And little Tabby," Daisy added.

Which was when it dawned on me.

Tabby? The cat was a *tabby* — and now that was its name, too!

The fairy I'd made friends with at ALD — was it her? Could it be? She'd told me she was starting a new job helping people through big life changes! It *had* to be her!

I stared at the kitten and tickled it under its chin. It looked up and lazily stretched its body into an arc.

Is it you? I asked silently. And I know I could have imagined it, but the kitten seemed to reply! It slowly opened an eye, stared straight at me, and winked.

I laughed out loud and shook my head. Maybe it *was* her; maybe it wasn't. It didn't matter. Suddenly, I didn't need to know all the answers. Things would unfold however they were meant to.

I looked at my two best friends and smiled. "D'you know what?" I said. "I've got the feeling everything is going to work out absolutely fine."

As if to agree with me, the kitten purred gently and stretched an arm out toward me, its tiny paw resting softly on my arm. And then it snuggled contentedly back down into Daisy's lap, curled into a fluffy ball, and went to sleep.

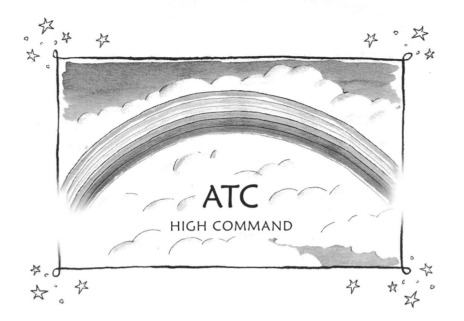

ATC

HIGH COMMAND

"Are you angry?" Alya asked.

"Not at all," Chara replied. "You?"

Alya shook her head. "Surprised?"

"Not even a tiny bit. As soon as she came back to ATC, I *knew* she'd find a way to get back to Earth."

Alya laughed. "Me, too." Then she wrinkled her forehead. "She will be all right, though, won't she?"

"Are you serious? She'll be absolutely fine. It even works out. I mean, without her powers, what could she do here, anyway?"

"Just—I mean, will she stay on Earth forever? Is that it? Is it all over for her as a fairy godmother?"

Chara smiled. As she did so, the light from a star high up in the sky shone down on the earth more brightly than any other. Even though it was the middle of the night, anyone who saw it had to shield their eyes.

"What?" she said. "After she's just made the kind of sacrifice only the most special fairy godmothers ever make?" She laughed lightly. "Oh, I doubt it."

Amber

This was it. I checked the address again. I definitely had the right place. It had taken weeks to track her down. It wasn't easy when I was constantly on call and sometimes had to rush back to the portal with a minute's notice.

But I'd done my research, and after about fifty dead ends, I was sure I had it this time.

I took a few deep breaths. What if she'd forgotten all about me? What if she thought I'd been a figment of her imagination? It had all been such a long time ago, and she'd been so young.

Should I back out?

I took another breath. No. She'd remember me. There was *no* backing out. I'd made a promise, and now, finally, I was going to keep it.

I waited until the receptionist at the elderly people's home had her back turned, then I slipped inside the door and whizzed through the foyer. I flew down the first corridor and around a corner. And then I saw it. Room 251. Her door.

My heart was beating even faster than my wings. The door was open. I could hardly breathe, I was so nervous. What if, what if . . .

Just do it.

I flew into the room. The old lady looked up and saw me. For a moment, she looked startled, taken aback. Shocked. And then her face broke out into the biggest, widest smile of recognition and joy that I could ever imagine seeing.

"Hello, Elsie," I said, smiling back at her. "Remember me?"

Once again, there are people I'm very lucky to have in my life who helped get this book from the idea in my head to the pages in your hands. Special thanks go to:

Linda Chapman, for always knowing what I'm trying to do with my stories and always helping me do it better;

Mary Hoffman, for coming up with the perfect title;

Jen Alexander, for introducing me to some of Cornwall's most beautiful stone circles;

The Scattered Authors' Society, for helping me grow as a writer;

Catherine Clarke, for always being there for every kind of support along the way;

Judith Elliott, for still and always being the best, nicest, most fun, and most supportive editor in the world;

Fiona Kennedy and everyone at Orion for being all-around wonderful;

Karen Lotz, Kate Fletcher, Tracy Miracle, and the whole team at Candlewick who have done such great things with my books;

And Laura Tonge, for being the perfect person to share a journey with — whether it's the journey of a van, a boat, a board, or a book!